CONDEMN ME NOT

ME NOT

Accused of Witchcraft

CONDEMN ME NOT

Accused of Witchcraft

HEATHER B. MOORE

USA Today Bestselling Author

Mirror Press

Interior design by Rachael Anderson
Edited by Jennie Stevens, Corey Pulver, and Lisa Shepherd

Cover design by Rachael Anderson
Cover image credit: Brekke Felt, Studio 15 Portraits
Cover model: Dana Moore, 11th great-granddaughter of Susannah Martin
Cover background: Adobe Stock #44827278 by Andreiuc88

Published by Mirror Press, LLC

ISBN-10: 1-9411-4595-7
ISBN-13: 978-1-9411-4595-1

A historical novel based on the life of
my 10th great-grandmother
Susannah North Martin

Accused of Witchcraft
Hanged in Salem, Massachusetts, in 1692

MY FAMILY LINEAGE

Susannah North Martin, born 1621

Abigail Martin, born 1659

Abigail Hadlock, born 1685

Rebecca A. Lowell, born 1708

Edmund Thurrell, born 1728

Moses Therrell, born 1750

Johnathan Therrell, born 1778

William Coker Lisonbee, born 1804

James Thompson Lisonbee, born 1839

Zina Lisonbee, born 1870

Scott R. Brown, born 1914

S. Kent Brown, born 1940

Heather Brown Moore, born 1970

Salem c. 1692

Amesbury

Salisbury

Merrimack

Newbury

Parker

Rowley

Atlantic
Ocean

Plum
Island

Ipswich

Ipswich

Cape Ann

Gloucester

Salem

Massachusetts
Bay

N

4 kilometers
4 miles

Created by Beehive Mapping

This woman was one of the most impudent, scurrilous, wicked creatures of this world; and she did now throughout her whole trial discover herself to be such a one. Yet when she was asked what she had to say for herself, her chief plea was that she had led a most virtuous and holy life.

—Reverend Cotton Mather, 1692

CHAPTER 1

Salem, Massachusetts 1692
Salem Jail

VEINS CRISSCROSS THE BACKS of my hands like a map of trails, intersecting, yet leading to nowhere—much like the path I've worn on the dungeon floor as I pace around the huddled bodies of women, carving footsteps into the cold, hard earth. Back and forth and around. Back and forth again, stopping at each wall, then passing the row of bars reaching from floor to the cragged ceiling.

Summer has yet to arrive in full, though the sound of birds can be heard in the first stretch of morning if I wake early enough and listen carefully above the sighing of female breath in sleep.

Rebecca Nurse prays in her sleep, her lips restlessly moving, as she talks to our Maker. I stop next to her and lean down as she whispers, "Lord, preserve our souls. Bless our accusers. O Lord . . ."

My eyes burn, and I straighten, as much as my seventy-one-year-old back can move.

The years have been harsh to my body, but that harshness seems like heaven compared to the squalor I live in now. Bearing eight children took its toll, yet I would bear eight more if I could but go home again to my George. But I cannot. He has been in heaven these past seven years.

Someone coughs, and it turns to a deep hacking sound. I wince as if the pain is pulsing through my own body. Rebecca sits up and hunches over as she coughs again, her hands to her mouth as her body shudders. I shuffle to the water bucket, the cords tied about my ankles chafing at my skin. I fill a ladle with stagnant water and kneel beside her.

"Take a drink, Rebecca," I say.

She lifts her head and smiles. That smile warms me through as no sun could ever do so before.

"Susannah, you are too good to me." Her voice is low and hoarse. She coughs again, and I rub her back as her body spasms. Rebecca is the same age as I—we are the two oldest women in the cell. Two of her sisters have also been accused and imprisoned, but they are not in our same cell. I hold the ladle close to her lips again. Finally, Rebecca is able to take a breath and drink.

"Thank you," she whispers, lying back on the ground with her eyes closed. She shifts her feet, causing the shackles about her ankles to clang together. Some of us have only cords to tie our ankles, since the prison had run out of shackles. Rebecca cracks one eye open. "Do you never sleep?"

"I woke to hear the birds," I say.

Rebecca coughs again, but I realize she is laughing. "The birds," she says. "I must thank the Lord for the birds." Her eyes close again, and her lips start to move in prayer.

I return the ladle to the bucket and cross to the only window in the dungeon. It sits high in the wall, a good foot over my head. If only I was tall like my mother, but I was a

2

small child and remained short into womanhood. The body parts that grew were my hips and breasts, and the latter George was more than happy for.

The sky is violet outside, and a faint rattle of the breeze pushes through trees that I cannot see. Leaning against the wall, I close my eyes. I hear better when I can't see—the wind, the birds, and sometimes I imagine I hear the grass drying under the warmth of the sun.

I have not felt the sun on my skin for nearly a month. May 2 was the date of my arrest, and now it is the first of June. The jailer announces the day each morning, otherwise I might not know what month or week it is. I marvel to think of the times I complained that the sun was too hot and that I ever regretted staying in the sun too long and burning my pale skin until it was bright pink.

George always had a bit of sunburn on his face, despite his hat, from working in the fields in the stark summer sun.

With my eyes closed, I could almost see him now, just like it was the first time. I used to watch him in the fields without his knowledge. His family moved to Salisbury when I was twenty-five, and when my stepmother heard that a family with an unmarried son bought the neighboring farm, she sent me over right away.

CHAPTER 2

I KNEW ALL THE single men in town, and none of them could be called a passing handsome. The verdict was still out on Orlando Bagley—a boy several years my junior, but I couldn't imagine marrying my best playmate.

Please, Lord, let the Martin boy be handsome, and un-wed . . . and about my age. I'd overheard my stepmother, Ursula, speaking to my father that week about finding me a husband. It was far past time, that I knew. At age twenty-five, I was becoming a disgrace. I guess the burden of my sassy mouth outweighed the virtual slave labor I did for her. When I heard the names of the men she suggested, my stomach twisted into a hard rock. Between Widower Parris with four children already and pimple-faced Bernard Allen, my choices were quite narrow. When not working on my parents' farm, I hired myself out as a nursemaid. My stepmother said I had a gift with healing. But she also thought it was a waste of my God-given time to sit by one of my brothers' or sisters' bedside as they lay sick.

"Susannah, pull the loaf out and wrap it in cloth for the Martins," my stepmother hollered from the kitchen. "Tell them I'll be over later with Father to make proper introductions."

I finished straightening the quilt on the bed of my sparse bedroom. At least I had it to myself since Mary had married Thomas Jones II and moved to Gloucester. My sister already had four children, one born before their marriage, and now Mary was pregnant again. I smoothed my hair back and twisted it into a tight bun, then pinned my white bonnet on.

Normally I'd complain about meeting the new neighbors on my own—but I wanted to be first to meet the unmarried man, to see for myself if he was anyone to be interested in. Besides, my stepmother wanted to be the first to greet the new family. If she delivered the first loaf of bread, we'd be considered the most neighborly—an important status in a Puritan community.

I stepped into the kitchen. The fire was fully roaring, heating up the big kettle of wash. Mother looked up at me, her face thin and flushed. "Hurry there and back. Today's washing day." My stepmother and I looked nothing alike, of course, so no one could mistake us for being related. Where she was tall and thin, I was short and on the stocky side. Although I could barely remember my own mother's looks, I was definitely my father's daughter.

I hurried as fast as I could across our fields without breaking a sweat. I'd put on a clean apron, one that was a bit too small, to show off the shape of my figure when tied tight around the waist. It was probably a sin to want to look like a woman in front of the Martin boy, but if he was handsome and single—without pimples and without a dead wife and little brats hanging on his legs—I'd ask the Lord to forgive me later.

I neared the border between the farms and picked my way around the fresh manure Father had laid that week. I didn't want to carry the smell of the farm when I reached the Martins' threshold. I was focusing so much on where not to step that I didn't see the plow until I nearly crossed in front of it.

"Whoa," a man said, stopping his horse that had been pulling the plow. It was a scrawny horse, not much better than ours. I wondered when my father had hired this laborer. He didn't mention it at supper last night, and I knew very well that we couldn't afford one. Father's back must really be in a bad way, even more than he let on to Mother. He must have hired this man from Salem or Gloucester, but why hadn't my father told me?

The man wore dark pants and a light-colored, long-sleeved shirt with no vest. That's when I noticed it was open in front, showing a bit of his chest, and that he was younger than I first thought.

He tipped up his hat and grinned. "Hello there." He was definitely younger than I thought. In fact, I guessed him at about three years my senior. Likely twenty-seven or twenty-eight. His dark blue eyes—maybe even gray—held mine. But I told myself not to stare at his eyes, or even think about the fact that he was handsome, despite the crook at the top of his nose. And I told myself that a man with such a wide smile couldn't be all that comely either. The Lord wanted men to be more modest around women and not to grin at them.

And I was definitely a woman.

"Do you speak English?" he said, studying me.

"Of course I speak English," I snapped, my shock at seeing this man made my tongue sharp.

He only chuckled at my outburst.

I took a step back, noticing that his boots were dark and

scruffy, but his hat was a light brown instead of black—maybe he wasn't from these parts. Maybe he wasn't even Puritan. I couldn't enter into a conversation with this stranger that made my blood hot. I needed to find a polite way to leave the man to his work.

"Are you Susannah North?" he said, and I stopped cold.

My father must have told this laborer my name—but why?—and then I looked past the stranger to the small house beyond the fields.

"Are you our new neighbor?" I asked, knowing the answer before he spoke.

He grinned and tipped his hat. "Yes, I'm George Martin. Pleased to meet you."

"And you," I said, barely able to speak coherently over the pounding of my heart. I had been openly gawking at him. Clearing my throat, I said, "I've come to meet your family."

George Martin's grin didn't waver. "My sister is inside the house. She'll be right pleased to meet you."

"Thank you," I said, and hurried around the plow, before giving him a chance to continue our conversation. Any Puritan male knew it wasn't proper to speak to unattended and unmarried women, which told me this man was nonreligious. What would my stepmother think of our new neighbors now?

Once I cleared the flanks of the horse, I hurried as fast as I could without breaking into a run, trying not to think of how his intense gaze had made my neck prickle. I crossed the border and cut to the lane leading to the house. Old Widow Framer used to live in this house until last winter, when she died of a disease of the lungs. At least that's what the physician said. Reverend said it was because she'd stopped paying her tithing. "Paying tithing is more important than eating. The spirit needs more nourishment than the body," he'd said.

I was panting by the time I reached the door. Surprised that it stood wide open, letting all manner of flies and bugs inside, I hesitated. Looking around, I saw no one and wondered if perhaps they'd gone to town to purchase supplies. Finally, I knocked. A woman's voice called out, "Come in."

It sounded raspy . . . and sick. I stepped inside and waited a few seconds for my eyes to adjust to the dimness. "Hello? Goody Martin?"

"In the back room," came the voice, fainter now.

I walked through the small house, taking note of the changes that had already taken place from when Widow Framer lived there. It was cluttered with crates piled into a corner, as if the Martin family was used to a larger home.

I pushed open the bedroom door that stood ajar. "Ma'am?" I said.

Two dark eyes peered at me over a worn quilt. The woman sat in a rocking chair, bundled in blankets. The woman looked to be in her mid-thirties, but her frailty made her seem older. She wore a white cap over her pale hair, and she was thinner than a bird. One hand darted out to wipe her mouth. "Come in, dear. That smells delicious."

I remembered the loaf of bread I carried, and I took a couple of steps forward. "I'm Susannah North, from the next property over."

"The Norths. Yes, the reverend told us you're our neighbors."

So the reverend had been here already. Did that mean they were religious after all? My stepmother wouldn't be too happy that the reverend had visited first. "Have you met anyone else besides the reverend?" I asked in a very innocent voice.

Her bird hand extended toward me. "No, dear. Come

closer and let me get a good look at you. My eyes aren't what they used to be. I've my brother to do most things for me now."

I shuffled a little closer and smelled rosemary. I wondered how sick this woman really was and why she was coddled up on such a nice warm day. The only ones in our town who spent their day in bed were those who were severely ailing. Or had just delivered a babe.

Her watery gaze assessed me quite shrewdly. "Are you the daughter who's yet unmarried?"

If I was a cursing woman, I would have cursed. Instead, I blushed. "That's me, ma'am."

A faint smile warmed her face. "George is my younger brother, not yet thirty. He was widowed this past year, God rest his wife's soul. But a man needs a wife, and although he's been too stubborn to marry yet, he should not remain unattached for long."

A widower . . . the man I'd met in the fields was a widower. And only just. Her eyes narrowed for a fraction as they studied me, as if to determine the level of my stubbornness as well. Then her face relaxed again. "My brother will be sorry he missed you. He's in town with the good sir, Mr. North. George is setting up an apprenticeship with the blacksmith there. I don't know what he sees in it—farming has been in our family for generations."

"I just met your brother," I said. "He must have returned early. I passed him working in the fields."

"Oh, wonderful," she said.

I wanted to move past the topic of her brother. "Is there anyone else in your family?"

"Alas, there's only us, and the small child of George's. I've never married on account of my health. Hannah is sleeping in the next room." Goody Martin brought her thin hand to her mouth and coughed. Then she continued as if her chest hadn't just been wracked in pain.

I listened to her talk about her niece, Hannah, and her childish antics. I wanted to ask more about George and what had happened to his wife. But I'd rather cut my hand with a butcher knife than ask such a thing. I took pity on this poor woman, stuck in her house with illness while her brother was out in the fresh air. I had so many questions, but instead I only asked, "Would you like me to slice a piece of bread for you?"

"That would be lovely," she said. "The knife should be unpacked and sitting out somewhere."

I left the bedroom and looked around the small kitchen, surprised at the orderliness in comparison to the first room I came through. Her brother must know how to set up a kitchen. Maybe they'd moved more than once. I wondered briefly what it would be like to live someplace other than Salisbury, but that was probably a sin, so I stopped wondering.

I found the knife and cut a slice of bread. There was a slab of butter covered with cheesecloth. I spread a thick layer of butter on the bread, deciding that Goody Martin needed all the fat she could get. After rewrapping the bread and leaving it on the table, I went back to the bedroom.

"You are such a dear." She took the lathered bread from me and nibbled at one end. "I'm sure your mother has a hard time sparing you. Tell me about your family."

So I told her about my real mother, who died back in England, and the new woman named Ursula my father married before leaving England. About how I was the youngest and how my stepmother lost two babies after me. I told her about my sister Mary and my other sister, Sarah Oldham, who at twenty-nine and widowed had vowed to never remarry. She and her twelve-year-old daughter, Ann, lived with us. I told her of all the babies my mother had who'd died: John, Hester, and Hepzibah.

Goody Martin exclaimed in all the right places, even saying, "Oh dear Lordy," a few times. I wasn't sure about that expression. It sounded Anglican to me.

"I shouldn't keep you long, but it's so nice to have a visitor," Goody Martin said, finishing the last of the bread. "Do you like to sew?"

Frankly, I was surprised she could eat the entire slice. "I sew," I said matter-of-factly.

She chuckled. "Yes, every good Puritan woman does."

I straightened my back a little at the compliment. It suited me fine.

"What does every good Puritan woman do?" a voice said behind me. I knew the voice, but I didn't want it to be the voice that I thought I knew.

"George! You're back so soon!" Goody Martin visibly straightened, and her face lit up like the morning sun.

He was here.

"I didn't go with Mr. North into town. When we headed out, I noticed that his field needed some plowing. And since the reverend told us of Mr. North's bad condition, I thought I'd put in a few lengths."

I turned to see George, my new neighbor.

"Hello there," he said, his eyes gleaming at me as if there was some big story behind them just waiting to get out. "I see you found my sister."

"Of course she did," Goody Martin said. "Why ever would you think she couldn't?"

George just grinned. My face heated hotter than a flame. Who was this man—this widower—shouldn't he have the dour countenance of a grief-stricken man? I clamped my lips together and turned back around, my eyes pleading to Goody Martin to not embarrass me. But she wasn't looking at me. Everything in her was focused on her brother.

"Susannah has brought us a fresh loaf of bread. She's the daughter of our new neighbors," she said. "The one yet unmarried."

If I thought I'd blushed before, I was sunset red now.

Goody Martin continued, "You can thank her kindly for the bread, instead of spouting nonsense." She shook her head at her brother. "You need to learn to treat a lady better. You've grown rusty, I own."

I refused to look at George again, although I could practically feel his eyes boring into my bonnet.

"We're obliged to you, Miss North," George said, and then he was standing near me. "My compliments to you. It smells like Heaven in here."

I had to look at him now, so close he stood. His eyes were gray, reminding me of storm clouds on a winter afternoon. I clenched my hand at my side. He grinned as he turned and left the room, presumably on his way to the kitchen for the bread.

I quickly made my farewell to his sister and hurried out, passing the kitchen without stopping. I was halfway out the door when George said, "Miss North, I can at least walk you to your property." He lowered his voice as if he didn't want his sister to overhear. "Practicing being a gentleman and all."

Instinct made me want to run out of the house and across the fields again, but now that this man was going to be my neighbor, I didn't want to do anything unchristian-like.

I folded my hands in front of me nice and proper and said, "That would be fine, sir."

He could hardly keep the grin from splitting his face open, and the mere sight of it made my heart thud. I was sure my face was red again.

"Thank you for the honor." He cast me a sideways glance. "And I promise to keep up a fine and suitable conversation as only a gentleman would."

As obnoxious as his words were, I felt a smile tugging at my mouth. But I kept my eyes down as I walked across the threshold. How could a widower be so cheerful?

George followed me.

I said nothing, and George talked. He told me about the small farm far north of Salisbury where they'd moved from. He told me about his brothers who had died, and his sister Alice, who lived in England and whom he hadn't heard from in years. And his sister Eve's illness, and how he'd taken care of her since the death of their mother.

Finally, I had to ask him a question. "How long has your sister been ill?"

"Since as long as I can remember. She cared for me as a small child, since our mother died when I was three, and once I became a man, I've cared for her ever since. It's like the life she led has dried up, and she tires very easily."

"And your wife?" I ventured to ask. The question was burning too hot to stay quiet.

"She died earlier this year in childbirth with our second child, who died as well."

I slowed my step, my heart growing heavy. "I'm very sorry," I said.

He nodded. "The child was born too early to survive."

We were both quiet for a moment. Childbirth brought all kinds of complications to a woman, and even though we were Puritans—chosen by God—the complications still came.

He'd suffered the loss of both a wife and child. All of my silly concerns seemed to disappear. I wished I had something wise or comforting to say.

But before I could say anything, he held up his hand. "I don't mean to damper the day. It's common knowledge enough."

"May God keep them," I said.

"Thank you," he said quietly.

We continued walking, this time in silence, and out of the side of my vision, I could see George watching me. Closely. I kept my focus on the lane, until I realized we'd reached the end.

"I appreciate the escort, sir," I said, hoping this was as far as he'd walk. I couldn't imagine what Mother would think if I showed up with George Martin at my side.

"*Sir*? That's what folks called my father. You may call me George."

I lifted my face to his and looked into his storm-cloud eyes. I felt as if I were just seeing a portion of what lurked behind his gaze. He was a grown man with a tragic history, yet here he stood, paying me with kindness, a soft smile on his face. "You may call me Susannah, then."

His gaze held mine until I could no longer stand it. I turned and hurried across the field so I didn't have to see his smile turn into a grin that I was already becoming familiar with.

I have often seen the apparition of Susannah Martin among the witches, but she did not hurt me till the 2 day of May being the day of her examination, but then she did afflict me most grievously during the time of her examination for if she did but look personally upon me she would strike me down or almost choke me . . .

—Elizabeth Hubbard, age 17

CHAPTER 3

Salem Jail

THE SLOP THEY BRING us is not fit for pigs. I wouldn't be surprised if the horses had turned away from it.

If the filth in the prison was not so deplorable, we could smell it coming. But as it is, the food arrives undetected. My hands join those of the other women as we reach for the rotted vegetables sloshing in bits of hay and fetid water. The time has long since passed that my stomach knots in anticipation. I focus on putting the food in my mouth and swallowing, hoping to live another day. Hoping that we will finish the food before the rats awake.

Hoping to see my children one more time. Six of my children are still living, as well as George's first daughter, Hannah.

It is the second of June, and I did not sleep much, as Sarah Good's babe fussed all night. Sarah has already been condemned to hang, but was pardoned until the birth of her child, fittingly named Mercy.

It appears they are both sleeping now, too soundly to even wake for the slop. I wonder who has paid for the food today. We are in prison with no means to earn money, yet we must purchase our own food and drink. Whatever a family member or friend buys for one of us, we all share with each other. I set aside a couple of decrepit tomatoes for Sarah. She keeps to herself for the most part; she is a brittle woman, not caring what others think of her. She's in her late thirties, thirty-nine perhaps, yet she looks years older. Even spending this past month in prison with her hasn't shown me her soft side. But I admire her all the same; she's been here since March. The warrant for her arrest was issued February 29, and since imprisonment she has refused to confess to witchcraft or accuse another—actions that would surely save her life.

The whole town has seemed to use her as a scapegoat, and although she continues to proclaim her innocence, she's made no overtures to be humble or conciliatory. When my trial comes, I hope to please the magistrates somehow, some way.

The babe whimpers, but Sarah does not stir. After a moment of fretting that the babe will release an all-out cry, I cross to the sleeping mother and lift the babe into my arms. She's a scrawny thing, born innocent to her circumstances. Sarah cracks a weary eye, and I half expect her to snatch her child back, but it seems exhaustion has won out, and she turns her head away and closes her eyes again. Next to Sarah sleeps her other daughter, four-year-old Dorothy, who was arrested on March 24 and taken to Ipswich jail, and then brought several days later to Salem.

The child is quiet and barely speaks. Only stays by her mother, continually scratches at the lice in her hair, and watches her care for the infant. My heart breaks yet fills with gratitude at the same time. At least I do not have a child in prison with me.

"You are too good to her," Elizabeth Howe says from her corner, her once smooth voice scratchy and hoarse, although she has only been in prison for a few days, since May 28. She's younger than most of us at age fifty-seven. Elizabeth is also a cousin to Rebecca Nurse.

"I cannot begrudge a turn of kindness," I say. The babe weighs almost nothing in my arms. I hope that when she's older, she'll not remember the conditions in which she was born.

I study Elizabeth Howe from my place. Out of all of us, she is the most cared for. Her daughters, Mary and Abigail, and other friends visit regularly, bringing country butter, food, and clean linen. Her husband, James Howe, comes with their daughters, and although he is blind, it's plain he is devoted as ever to his wife. Despite these apparent luxuries, Elizabeth is as destitute as the rest of us in mind and soul.

I rock the babe, looking into the child's pale blue eyes. What can be going through this infant's mind? Does she have any comprehension that she was born in a prison cell? That her mother will be executed?

I am not surprised at Sarah Good's possessiveness with the babe. Not even the rats or lice dare bother her child. I cannot even bear to look over at little Dorothy, who quietly whimpers in her sleep. I can't imagine anyone so cruel as to accuse a child of witchcraft, let alone hang her. But the longer I am in this prison, the less faith I have in our magistrates.

I wonder how long they will let Sarah live and care for her baby. Every day with the babe is one day closer to Sarah's death. And what will become of little Dorothy and her sister? Will the other women in prison adopt the children? Will they be sent to a foster family? The babe is smaller than any of my children at that age. It's no wonder, due to the lack of nourishment and fresh air—a child needs sunlight.

I am grateful my children are grown and have not been implicated in my accusations. The women in the cell might think I'm crazy if I tell them that my George has made sure of that, somehow, from his place in heaven. But holding little Mercy tears at my heart. What sort of future does this child have? I am so caught up in considering the babe's circumstances that I do not hear the shuffling steps of the prison guard.

His voice startles me. "Goody Martin. You have been called up for examination."

My heart drops. I knew my time would come, but from the expressions on the other women's faces, they fear for me. It is not a formal trial yet, but an examination that will determine whether or not I go to trial.

Dread rushes through me, and I realize that although I've been in this cell for weeks, I do not feel prepared to face the magistrates.

Rebecca starts to pray, and I take courage in that. Elizabeth rises to her feet and takes the babe. In the opposite corner, Sarah Wildes, a woman in her mid-sixties and imprisoned since April 21, lifts her head. The fear in her eyes reflects my own.

The cell door lumbers open, and I brush at my filthy skirt. There is no use in trying to make myself presentable. I do not even have clean water, let alone a mirror or a comb. I follow the prison guard, walking past other cells, filled with other men and women awaiting trial.

I'm thankful for the guard's pace because my seventy-one-year-old body has slowed, and more considerably in the past weeks. I have lost weight, and my normally full figure has already shrunk. I have been hungry since the day I arrived, but it's not the starvation that brings me the most pain, it's being separated from my family.

The jailer leads me into another room. Ten pairs of eyes settle on me, belonging to nine women and the surgeon John Barton, the man in charge of the witches' examinations. My heart sinks at the sight of the surgeon and the jury of women.

Did I expect the girls and women who accused me to be watching and waiting to confess more lies such as those told by Abigail Williams and Elizabeth Hubbard on that awful day last month when I was first convicted and brought before Judge Hathorn and Judge Corwin? I was questioned extensively on May 2 in front of a court full of people, and I couldn't help but laugh when the afflicted girls began to have fits. The magistrate did not take too kindly at my laughter about the folly of the girls.

And although I adamantly maintained my innocence, my prison cell has been home since.

The jailer directs me to the front of the room, and then he turns to leave. "I will collect the others."

Others? I stand in the middle of the room, feeling the weight of the stares around me like an anchor slowly dragging me down.

One by one, the jailer escorts in four more women: Rebecca Nurse and Sarah Good from my cell, and Alice Parker and Elizabeth Proctor. We are a pathetic group of prisoners. Women who should be at home and on their farms taking care of their families. Instead, we are kept away from all civilization.

"Goody Martin, do you know why you stand for examination today?" asks John Barton, drawing my attention. It seems that since I'm the first to arrive, I am the first to be examined.

I nod, then say, "I have committed no sin nor crime. I am here because I am obeying the law."

Barton's face flushes, and he looks down at the official document he holds. "There are methods which are used to determine whether or not a person is indeed a witch."

I know. I've heard of convictions made from when these methods are proved useful, although I deem them ridiculous.

"Remove your clothing so that we might see if you have grown a witch's teat."

I stare at the man and wonder if I've heard right. Perhaps I've fallen asleep in the cell and am now dreaming.

The jailer, who has remained in the room with us, steps forward, the look on his face determined.

"If you do not remove your clothing," Barton continues, "we will do so for you."

My gaze flits to the female jurors. Only a few of them will meet my eyes. Sitting on the bench against the wall are the other prisoners. I feel their own shock radiate toward me. I can't quite comprehend the request. I had thought the humiliation over. Not even my children have seen me without clothing—the only soul on earth since I was a child has been my husband. Now, these strange men and women are asking me to remove my clothing?

I take a step back, not realizing what I may be doing. "You can't mean your request. I do not have a witch's teat." I look from Barton to the women jurors, but there is no softening in their faces.

Barton's words are firm. "If you do not have a witch's teat, then you will need to prove it to us."

The jailer moves toward me, and I have enough sense to raise my hand and motion for him to stop. I unbutton my dress with trembling hands, then fold it once and let it drop to the floor. I already feel exposed, and I am not yet naked. My stomach clenches, and I can no longer look into the eyes of the peering men.

24

I slide off my shift and am left with only my intimate underthings of cotton. Every part of my body feels scorched with shame and embarrassment, and I want to heave up the rotted vegetables churning in my stomach.

A cold chill spreads across my chin as I remove the final pieces of clothing. And then I am standing in the middle of the examination room, the surgeon, the jailer, and nine female jurors staring at me, as I wear nothing. The other prisoners have lowered their heads, certainly dreading their turns.

Even as a young woman, I was conscious of my figure. I was never as thin as the other girls my age, and it wasn't until I married George that I felt any semblance of beauty. Perhaps it was just because he was George and he loved me, but I decided my body could please him and that I wouldn't worry about my curves.

But now, I hate my aged body. I hate my nakedness, and I hate what these men and women must see. But most of all, I hate that they are now looking at what I have only reserved for my husband.

My eyes close because I can't bear to see them looking at me. But then they fly open as I hear movement. By God, they are coming toward me. Each one takes a turn walking around me, and my body is hot and cold at the same time. Mostly it is cold, but my heart hammers with hatred fiercer than I've ever felt before.

These men and women might examine me, but they will not find any damned witch's teat, and they will not coerce me to accuse any other woman. No matter who has been an enemy in the past, I would never subject them to this.

Mr. Barton pays particular attention to my breasts, and then everyone is shuffling back to the bench. "You may dress," Mr. Barton says as my eyes blur with tears.

CHAPTER 4

Salisbury

MOTHER AND I LOADED the cart for market day. My niece, Ann, scurried around us, loading as fast as she could. She was looking forward to seeing her friends. Her mother, Sarah, would be staying home again. Sarah wasn't much for social gatherings, and sometimes she wouldn't even go to church—claiming an upset stomach—but I knew better.

We were taking tomatoes and squash from our garden, hoping to get enough earnings to purchase wheat. We'd nearly run out of last year's store, having had to sell most of it to get us through the winter. If there was one thing to look forward to on market day, it was seeing my sister Mary. Since she'd moved to Gloucester with her husband, I'd missed her.

The scent of spring was sharp in the air, and as I gazed across our land, I had to admire the fine job of plowing that George Martin had done. He'd helped my father more than he could ever know, and my father's pride had managed to stay intact.

"George Martin has requested that I help them refurbish their well," my father had said, reverence in his voice. He'd been a brick mason in England, but hadn't been able to work in that profession as he once did. Keeping up the farm was a day-and-night task.

But for my father, it was more than a fair trade for a plowed field.

I felt a bit of a soft spot toward George myself, but only because he'd helped my father, not for any other reason. Besides, I was sure that once George was seen at Meeting on the Sabbath, he'd have a dozen and one women after him—all younger than me, likely prettier, and much more agreeable.

"Susannah!" Mother said, startling me. "Where are your thoughts today? They'd better be with the Lord, or there's no sorry excuse that I'll accept—"

"Sorry." I straightened the square of hide that was draped over the vegetables to keep them protected from the sun, then tugged at the rope Mother had tossed over me. Once it was secured on my end, she gave it a final tug on hers.

"Let's go," Ann said, her impatience clear as she practically bounced on the wagon seat. Her light brown hair had been pulled into a single braid that was already fraying.

Mother studied me. "Isn't there a cleaner dress you can wear? We'll see the whole town today."

"Of course," I said, not arguing, although it mortified me that she scolded me in front of Ann. My gray pinafore was clean and pressed, but I wasn't too interested in making an impression on . . . anyone. When I looked down at my apron, I saw the wisdom in Mother's request.

I hurried inside the house and pulled the clean pinafore from its peg. Then I spent a little extra time in front of the polished brass mirror. Father thought it was vain to even have the thing in the house, but Mother insisted that we needed to look neat and tidy, and what happened if no one was at home to do the inspection?

So it was looking into the brass that I unraveled my two braids and finger-combed my hair until it hung in soft waves down my back. Vain, indeed, but I no longer looked like a school girl. Even at the age of twenty-five, I appeared to be in my teens. Maybe it would be a blessing when I was an elderly woman, but for now, it was merely an inconvenience.

"Tell Mary hello for me," Sarah said, coming into the room. She looked better than she did a short time ago when she told Mother she wasn't feeling well. My suspicions were confirmed.

"I will," I said. "She'll be staying the night so her family can go to Sabbath services with us."

Sarah gave a faint smile. Her hair was the same brown as her daughter, Ann's, although Sarah's lacked any warmth that would have come from the sun if she'd spent any time outside. "All the better to enjoy peace and quiet for a bit before everyone arrives."

I was about to agree when my mother's voice came from outside. "Susannah!"

"Coming," I called and grabbed my straw hat. A bonnet would flatten the waves in my hair. I said good-bye to Sarah, and when I reached the wagon, Mother glanced at me, but said nothing.

I didn't know why I worried about what my hair looked like on this day, but my heart was fluttering like mad by the time we reached the market. It might have had something to do with the wagon I saw up ahead. It was too far to catch up to, but it definitely carried the Martin family.

In the past couple of days, I'd seen George in the fields from a distance. I had yet to see his young daughter, Hannah.

Mother noticed my gazing. "The Martins seem to be a nice family. George seems plenty strong, although his sister ails. He was widowed earlier this year, left with a young daughter, poor man. She died birthing their second child. I expect he's looking for a wife now."

I stiffened, remembering what George had told me. I found something else to gaze at. It wasn't hard to guess where my mother's mind was. I'd told her about Goody Martin, and Mother had been there to visit herself since that first day, but she was much more interested in discussing George and whether or not he was Puritan.

Before I could slow the wagon down, I realized that George had stopped up ahead of us. He had hopped out and was inspecting the back wheel.

I automatically reined in our horse, slowing down. "Whoa, Chip." By the time I pulled alongside their wagon, George was kneeling in the dirt. He'd removed his jacket, and his broad shoulders strained against the linen of his shirt. It appeared that Goody Martin needed to cut a bigger cloth for her brother.

Quickly averting my gaze as George turned and looked up at us, I stared ahead as Mother said, "Can we give you a ride the rest of the way? You could bring back tools to make the repair."

I felt George's gaze on me. "That would be generous of you, ma'am," he said, "but I don't think your wagon has extra room."

I looked at him then and could see he was holding back a smile. Beside me, Ann giggled. She, apparently, was charmed by him.

"Nonsense, you can fit up front with us. Ann can sit among the baskets for a short time," Mother said, not letting it drop.

There was barely room enough for two adults and a child on the bench, let alone three adults.

"I don't mind walking, ma'am," George said, then looked at Ann and gave her a wink.

She giggled again, and I felt my face grow hot.

"Mr. Martin," Mother started, "Neighbors help neighbors around here. The sun will be too hot soon, and you'll likely get hungry." What George didn't know was that Mother didn't take no for an answer. Ann scrambled into the back of the wagon and found a perch. Mother scooted over to the farthest side of the bench, so I was forced to move right into the middle, which meant when George climbed into the wagon, he sat next to me.

"Much obliged, Mrs. North," he said, tipping his hat.

It reminded me of when I'd first met him in the field. But I kept my body stiff and my eyes forward as I urged our horse forward.

The wagon lumbered on for a few paces, then George said, "You've a fine horse there, Mistress North."

I choked. *Fine horse?* Was he jesting? The wagon jarred over a rut, and George's shoulder connected with mine. Even though the wagon ride was bumpy enough, I had the feeling George had done it on purpose.

"Chip's an old horse, had him since Susannah was young," Mother said.

Do not tell George my age. Do not, Mother, I wanted to shout.

"Susannah, how old were you when we got him?"

"I don't remember," I muttered, knowing that my mother was just postulating.

"About fifteen? So that would make Chip about ten?"

I wanted to disappear—completely—and never appear again. I could imagine George adding fifteen and ten right now. We hit another rut, and George bounced against me. I bit back a curse. My mother had told me the more I cursed, the longer the Lord would wait to send me a husband.

I was fine with waiting.

But I didn't want to live with my parents the rest of my life either.

We neared the town center, and I slowed the wagon and found a good place to set up. Ann scrambled off the wagon and ran over to see a friend across the square. George hopped down from the bench and walked around and helped my mother down. Then he was back at my side before I could climb out. He held his hand up, his blue-gray eyes on me, his mouth a slight smile.

He was laughing at me, I knew it. A spinster who couldn't even get a civil word out.

I stayed in my place, holding his gaze. He stayed in his, hand still outstretched.

"Susannah, let the man help you down," Mother said from the other side of the wagon.

My face flamed, and George chuckled. Were they in cahoots with each other?

Reluctantly, I let go of the reins and put one hand in his, barely touching it. But his fingers closed over mine, strong and warm. He tugged me toward him, practically making me fall out of the wagon. When I landed on my feet, his other hand grasped my waist.

"Whoa," he said.

"I'm not a horse."

One of his brows lifted. I was standing much too close to him. Surely he had dirt on his clothes from kneeling on the ground, and I didn't relish the thought of soiling my clean pinafore.

"I agree. You're nothing like a horse."

I tilted my head up. He didn't smell like the other farmers I'd been around. Perhaps he'd bathed this morning. I appreciated his sweet musky scent, then remembered that I wasn't going to appreciate anything about him. Not someone who laughed at me.

"Susannah," he said, his voice low.

Something shivered through me in anticipation.

"Did you know your eyes are the color of new wheat?"

I stared at him for a second, then blinked. "You think I look like wheat?"

He grinned—that same grin I'd tried to forget—and my heart thumped.

Before he could reply, I'd pulled away from him and walked to the back of the wagon. Mother lowered her gaze—she'd seen the interchange, but how much she'd heard, I didn't know. Yet I knew it was enough. Her face had softened into a smile.

In the latter end of April 1692 there appeared to me the Apparition of a short old woman which told me her name was Goody Martin and that she came from Amesbury who did most grievously torment me by biting and pinching me, urging me vehemently to write in her book, but on the 2 May 1692 being the day of her examination Susannah Martin did torment and afflict me most grievously . . .

—Mercy Lewis, age 19

CHAPTER 5

Salem Jail

ALL IS QUIET AS the women around me nap when I hear the sound of slow and steady footsteps, and because my heart leaps I know it's George. He's come to see me more than once, although I cannot admit it to the other women. George has been dead for years, so I am not sure how to explain his visits. Perhaps they'd think I am a witch after all, summoning the dead.

But whether or not it's my imagination or George has come in spirit form, my heart syncs to the rhythm of his steps as he approaches the cell. He's tall and hasn't aged since the day I kissed him good-bye on his deathbed.

The lines on his face remind me of my own lines, and his eyes are the same eyes I've been looking into since the day we met. Their grayness settles on me, and I cross the cell to speak to him.

"Susannah," he says in a soft, low voice. His hand reaches for mine through the bars.

I grasp the warmth—imagined warmth that I believe in.

"Your hands are cold," he says, and I nod, lowering my head. More than just my hands are cold. My entire body is chilled with the eyes of the men who examined me. It is all I can do to stand upright and not shake in front of George.

His other hand comes through the bars, wrapping around my waist, as if it is possible to embrace with metal between us.

Still, I press against the bars and wish that I could hold him close. I breathe in his fresh scent, one of the golden sun and blue sky and green fields. I know I must smell of dank and rot, but perhaps he doesn't notice those things anymore. Can angels smell humans? His shoulders are no longer the muscled ones of our early marriage, but they are strong and have seen decades of blacksmithing. Hard work to provide for our children.

This thinner, older man is still my George.

"I wish I could bring you something to eat," he says.

"Let's pretend you have," I say.

If he had really brought bread, the women in my cell would have awakened immediately and demanded I share.

"Thank you for coming," I whisper. My voice seemed to flee after my appearance before the court. Even though I remained strong under their scrutiny, I can feel my courage failing now. I do not tell George this. I do not tell him what I've endured this morning, and I can only pray that he did not see it for himself.

"The children can put our land up against your charges. You must send a message."

"No," I say. "I don't want them near the courts." George and I have not had good luck with the courts. Soon after our marriage, Widow Leeds's accusation against me led to a fine of twenty shillings and loss of my Meeting seat placement.

Some years later, in 1669, William Sargent Jr. accused

me of being a witch. Charges were eventually dropped after George sued both William Sargent and Thomas Sargent. But then soon after, George was sued by Christopher Bartlett, all because I had called him a liar and a thief—which was true.

The day we went to the Salisbury court to face Bartlett, my son Richard was also tried for abusing my George. It was little more than a tantrum. Regardless, Richard was found guilty and was sentenced to ten lashes with the whip.

Our large family had its own fair share of challenges, but after my father's death in 1667, we discovered that my stepmother, Ursula, had altered his will only weeks before he died. His complete estate had been willed to Ursula. My sister Mary was left with five pounds, I with twenty shillings and ten pounds, and my niece Ann Bates with five pounds. My other sister, Sarah, died a few years after I married George.

When Ursula died a few years later, she left the estate to Mary's daughter, Mary Jones Winsley. And for the next three years, we battled the courts, and finally, we lost the case and I lost my inheritance.

"You cannot stay here," George says, his eyes stormy.

Have my children tried to barter our land in Amesbury for my freedom? Is that why I was so thoroughly examined? It's true that the constable benefits from the accused witches. He goes into the homes and claims whatever property he wants. Who knew that witchcraft accusations could be so lucrative? George cannot know about the examination. He cannot know the price I have paid.

I thread my fingers through his, wishing I was out of this hellhole and kneeling at his graveside. I vow to bring flowers every day, if only to be outside, surrounded by nature, close to my husband's final resting place in Amesbury.

This, here, is not how I expected to live my later years. I should be with my husband, sitting on our rockers and visiting with our grandchildren. Isn't that how the elderly are supposed to pass their twilight years?

"Esther has nearly finished your quilt," he tells me.

Tears burn in my eyes. George has been watching over our children, and now Esther has been working on the quilt I'd started before my prison sentence. To think that I was frustrated by the quilt's complicated pattern, borrowed from Goody Stone. And to think that my stubborn, willful daughter finally had the patience to finish it.

"I can't wait to see it," I say, trembling.

"So you shall . . . so you shall," George says, pressing his lips against my forehead.

But I do not want any of my children to come here, to this place. I know they pay money to send food, but I cannot let them see me. I lean into him for a moment, remembering a past time and place, and how he used to hold me at night, his arms warm and strong about me. Always making me feel safe.

Here, in the prison, I no longer feel safe. A jury of women and a surgeon have examined my naked body.

I feel like the speck of dust beneath my feet.

I reach up to stroke my husband's face. He might fade away at any moment. This dear man has been at my side through everything: the birth of our eight children, the death of his sister, the death of my parents. Our move to Amesbury. The first time I was accused of witchcraft. The court battles over my father's property.

And always, he has been there. He has loved me. He has cared for me, just as he promised.

At first, I pay little attention to the approaching footsteps, assuming they belong to a family member of another woman in the cell.

"Goody Martin, you're requested for another examination." It is the jailer.

My body stiffens. Again? What more do they need? What more can they ask?

George steps back, his eyes on the jailer, and although he does not speak to me when others are listening, I know what he's asking. "*Another* examination? What's happened, Susannah?"

I can't quite meet his eyes. It is too horrific to tell, and to try to soften the truth will not work with George. I cannot lie to him. His hand reaches through the bars to touch mine.

I step back so that the jailer can let me out of the cell. Then I am free, for the few moments of walking along the prison corridor, on the other side of the bars for once.

I say nothing to George; I don't want to give the jailer any reason to add to my accusations.

"Come along," the jailer says.

George's hand brushes mine as I walk past him.

And that is what gives me the courage to follow the jailer into the examination room again. I wonder what questions will be asked; what more can they want to know? Will they believe me anyway? The Salem prison is full of women whom they choose not to believe. How will I be any different?

It's like a recurring nightmare when I step again into the examination room. The only difference is that the light has shifted from morning to afternoon. The same juror of matrons are there along with Mr. Barton. I wait as the jailer brings in Bridget Bishop, Rebecca Nurse, and Elizabeth Proctor. I wonder briefly about Sarah Good, but I am also relieved she is being spared for now.

I am again asked to remove my clothing. I want to collapse to the ground and bury myself right there. What cruel fate is this?

This time, instead of feeling like stone inside, heat pulses through me—embarrassment, humiliation, anger. Hot tears course down my face, dripping off my jaw and landing on my bare breasts.

The surgeon and the matrons speak to each other about my body, about what they see, as if I am not there, but a standing corpse to be examined.

"Her breasts are slack," one woman says. I've closed my eyes and do not see which one is speaking.

"Yes," another voice comes. "They were full this morning."

Full? I am seventy-one years old and have nursed eight babies. My breasts have not been full for decades.

I hear the scratch of a quill upon rough paper. Mr. Barton is writing down their observations of my breasts. I want to throw up.

"A demon will suckle any teat," one of the women says. "It appears she's been busy while in prison."

My hands clench into fists, and I open my eyes. My breasts are the same as they've always been. They are the breasts of a woman who is aged and spent her life raising babies. They represent what God gave me to nourish my children through infancy. How dare these people call them devil's teats.

I am shaking, ready to scratch their eyes out. It will be a fitting end to the month of hell I've spent in prison. The gossip will spread through town like wildfire—*Goody Martin, overcome by the devil, attacks the magistrates.*

I force my mind toward my children and grandchildren. I haven't told them good-bye. My hands slowly unclench as I think of my family and what they'd do if I didn't return to them.

I don't want to bring them more pain than I already

have. The accusations against me have brought enough ugliness into our lives.

I exhale as the matrons settle onto their bench. Then I quickly dress, and as I tremble before them, Mr. Barton reads the verdict. "Enough evidence has been found on Susannah North Martin, accused of witchcraft, to move forward with a trial. On June 26, 1692, she will appear in this court and stand trial for witchcraft."

June 26. Three weeks.

I am as good as guilty. No man or woman has been released who did not confess to witchcraft and accuse others. Unless I confess to a crime that I did not commit, I will be sentenced to death. The irony does not escape me. Lying before God will buy my freedom among men.

I lean against the wall, trying not to collapse as the other women are told to undress and their examinations take place. There is an argument between the surgeon and one of the matrons as they discuss the odd excrescence of flesh on Rebecca Nurse's privates. When she tells them about her difficult births, Mr. Barton seems mollified.

When the examinations are finished and as the jailer escorts me back to the prison, I try to forget the looming trial date. The jailer leads me down the prison steps, and I imagine George standing there, waiting for me. But, of course, he is not. With every step closer to the cell, my chest tightens.

All too soon, I'm locked in the cell again, and tears are falling down my face.

I say nothing, but watch the jailer walk away from me. Just before he steps out of view, he looks back at me, and I see the pity. If there is one thing I cannot abide, it's pity.

CHAPTER 6

Salisbury

THE MARKET WAS ALREADY teeming with people before we had the chance to get fully set up. George had disappeared among the throng, in search of tools to borrow. It seemed that all of Salisbury had turned out, as well as others from surrounding towns. Ann returned to our wagon to help arrange the garden produce we were selling, then she disappeared again, walking with one of her friends. Everyone seemed excited to be out and catching up with the latest news.

"Susannah!" My sister's voice cut through the throng. Mary hurried toward me, as much as she could hurry. Her growing belly slowed her down somewhat, but she was still more petite than me. Her blonde hair was tied neatly back from her face, and she wore a colorful shawl around her shoulders. She looked positively like a spring day. Two of her children, little Susanna and Thomas, followed her, as she balanced baby Mary on her diminishing hip.

I'd seen her in various stages of her other pregnancies, and she had never been so large and cumbersome this early before. The baby wasn't due until the fall, and already she looked peaked.

I embraced her and the children, then settled back onto the hitch of the wagon. Little Susanna and Thomas scurried under the wagon to play and stay out of the sun.

"Where's your husband?" I asked.

"He's over talking to Mr. Brown." She peered at me. "Your hair looks pretty that way." She shifted baby Mary to her other hip. I reached out and took the child from her, if only to give her a small rest.

Baby Mary patted my face, then leaned against my neck, her soft curls a caress against my hot skin.

"I thought a change would be nice," I said, thinking that changing the subject would be ideal. Mary was much too observant for her own good. "How are *you* feeling?"

Her smile lit up her fair face. "Much better now that I'm in the sixth month. Joyce gave me something that helps with the aches." Her hand went to her extended belly. "Some days my skin hurts like it's stretching something fierce. Thanks for holding baby Mary. She's been wanting to nap."

Joyce was a woman who lived not too far from Mary's house in Gloucester. I had met her on the occasion of my visits to see Mary. But she was also an odd one, muttering to herself as she worked in her herb garden. "Be careful, you hear," I warned Mary. "I don't know if I'd take something prepared by Joyce's own hands."

"She's harmless," Mary said. "Besides, it's helping, and I'm not one to complain about having energy for my chores."

I pulled her hands toward me and turned them over. "Any pock marks?"

"Of course not," she said, tugging her hands away with a laugh.

"What are you talking about?" Mother interrupted.

"I was just showing Susannah that my hands are swelling like a pig," Mary said.

I stifled a laugh, and my sister cast me a conspiratorial smile. *Oh Lord, forgive us for lying to our mother.*

But Mother didn't seem to notice anything was amiss, and I looked over at her to see why her attention was diverted. George Martin was striding toward us.

"Who is *that?*" Mary said under her breath, nudging me.

I elbowed her back. "Hush. I'll tell you later."

George stopped before my mother. "Thank you again for your assistance, Mrs. North."

"You're welcome. I hope you got the wagon repaired."

"That I did," George said, his gaze sliding to me and the babe I held. He looked over at my sister, then back to me.

Mother made no effort to introduce Mary, but said instead, "Be sure to give your sister our best. I'll visit her on the morrow."

George nodded and made his farewell. We all watched him walk away.

Before Mary could pry for information, Mistress Beedle came by and inquired after Mary's health. She politely answered her questions, then when Mistress Beedle turned to our mother, Mary leaned over to me.

"Did you see how he looked at you?" she whispered because baby Mary had fallen asleep on me. "You must tell me his name."

I refused to blush. "It's George Martin. His family moved into Widow Framer's place. He's looking to apprentice as a blacksmith in town . . . and he wasn't looking at me."

Mary scrunched her nose. "No wonder you aren't married. You don't even see a good thing when it's looking right at you."

"How do you know he's a good thing?" I asked. "Did you know he's widowed? With a young daughter?"

I could still see George on the other side of the square. He'd stopped to talk to someone I didn't recognize.

"If you have to ask that, then you are completely blind," Mary said. "And if you don't snatch him up, then someone else will."

Anabel Temple joined the men—now I knew who George was speaking with. Her uncle was from Marblehead. He'd been in town before. It was plain that her uncle was now introducing Anabel to George. Did the men know each other already? "Well, it looks like it's too late."

Mary grimaced, watching the introductions. "Anabel is nothing compared to you. If he chooses her, he's a dumb wit."

"Anabel is younger, prettier, thinner, and blonder . . . not to mention wealthier than me. How is there even a comparison?"

My sister smiled. "Oh, you *do* care, don't you?"

"I didn't say that. All I said was—"

"It doesn't matter what you said," Mary cut in. "It's what I heard."

I scoffed, refusing to speak another word to her until she decided to have a reasonable conversation. Mary laughed and moved over to talk to my mother and Mistress Beedle. I leaned against the wagon, cradling baby Mary in my arms as she slept against my neck. Perhaps my sister was right. She certainly had more experience than I with men; she had a husband and children.

George and Anabel were still in my line of vision, and they were still talking. Anabel made no pretensions that she was enamored with whatever he was saying. I wondered what interesting thing he could be discussing that would keep her so captivated. Usually, Anabel acted like she was too good for the young men in Salisbury. She talked about marrying someone from Salem because the pickings were slim here.

It seemed the pickings had just grown by one.

My stomach churned as I watched the two talking. *Don't be ridiculous.* I didn't even know George, and he was too conceited anyway for my taste. Plus, he was probably interested in younger women and would make himself scarce now that he knew my real age. Not that I thought there was a chance he was interested in me—at least not now. I might have been the first woman he met in Salisbury, but I'd definitely not be the last.

"You're better than she is," Mary was saying. "Do you want me to bring my old clothes on next market day? My green dress will be a nice one for Sabbath. George will notice you in that."

"Your clothes don't fit me," I said sharply, embarrassed at having been caught staring at George and Anabel. Mary was taller and thinner than me, except when she was pregnant.

"The dress might be a touch tight, but maybe that's even better," she said conspiratorially.

I jabbed her with my elbow, and she held back a laugh.

I pulled my hair back into the fiercest bun, and I wore my pale gray dress and dark gray bonnet. Today was Sabbath, and my family was preparing to go to Meeting.

As I stepped outside, Mary's family was already loaded in their wagon.

"You're early," I said, crossing to the wagon.

Mary brushed a strand of hair from her face. She looked tired, although it was only morning. "I hardly slept last night, so I packed everything up early. We'll save you a place next to us." She narrowed her eyes. "You look like you're going to a funeral."

I shrugged. "So be it."

She studied me for a moment. "You're not fooling me, Susannah. There's a man you're interested in, and even if you cut off your hair and dressed like a boy, he'd still notice you."

I folded my arms and said nothing.

Mary squeezed my arm and chuckled. Then she turned away, and let her husband help her lumbering form into the wagon. I watched them drive away, then I turned back toward the house.

The past couple of days, I'd seen George Martin helping my father with planting. Apparently, they were great friends now, as well as best neighbors.

And Mother was humming every minute she wasn't singing.

I waited on the porch for the rest of the family, enjoying the fresh air. When my mother came out of the house, she stopped and admired the sown fields. "That George Martin sure does good work."

Father came up behind her, adjusting his hat. "That he does."

Both of my parents looked at me expectantly. "What do you think, Susannah?" Mother asked.

I shrugged. "Well, he is a man, and he's used to farm labor, it seems." Some days I didn't see him at all and assumed he was in town with the blacksmith.

"You should be more respectful and thank the Lord for George Martin's generosity," Mother said.

A slight smile touched Father's face. I wasn't sure what he was smiling about. I expected him to agree with everything Mother said anyway; I couldn't remember a time when he hadn't.

"I think George Martin is nice," Ann said, coming out of the house with her mother.

Sarah gave one of her rare smiles and squeezed Ann's hand. "We'll get Susannah hitched soon enough."

I folded my arms, not liking the entire family on the same side against me. "I think I'll walk to Meeting today."

"Nonsense," Mother said. "You'll be late if you walk, and you don't want to arrive all sweaty."

Mother was right, although if I'd have known our conversation was going to be centered on George Martin, I would have planned to set out earlier for Meeting.

My father climbed into the wagon and took a moment to get situated. He grimaced, but hid it well—it must be a painful day for him. He never complained, but I heard his moans at night when my mother rubbed out his back so that he could sleep.

I swallowed down the guilt of my earlier retort. I should be grateful that George was helping with the planting—it was a blessing to my father and to all of us. But why did it have to be a man whose blue-gray eyes made my heart pound?

I hadn't allowed myself to think much about him, at least when I was busy doing other things, and, if I did, only once in a while. I climbed up in the wagon and sat in the back. The Martins would surely be at Meeting, and everyone in the town would be interested in getting to know them. Anabel wouldn't be the only one fawning over George.

One or two and thirty years ago Elizabeth my wife being a very rational woman and Sober and one that feared God as was well known to all that knew her and as prudently careful in her family, which woman going upon a time from her own house towards the mill in Salisbury did there meet with Susannah Martin the then wife of George Martin of Amesbury. Just as they came together Susannah Martin vanished away out of her sight which put Elizabeth into a great fright. After which time Martin did many times afterward appear to her at her house and did much trouble her in any of her occasions and this continued till about Feb, following, and then when she did come it was as birds pecking her legs or pricking her with the motion of their wings and then it would rise up into her stomach with pricking pain as nails and pins of which she did bitterly complain and cry out like a woman in travail and after that it would rise up to her throat in a bunch like a pullet's egg and then she would turn back her head and say, witch you shan't choke me.

—William Browne, age 70

CHAPTER 7

Salem Jail

SARAH GOOD CRIES IN her sleep tonight, and her babe is restless as well. Silent as always, Dorothy sleeps next to her, never giving any protest. When I try to approach Sarah and comfort her, she only lashes out. She has what we call prison-rot. It's what happens when someone finally breaks. It can happen within hours of first coming to the cell, or it may take weeks.

I think I've been on the verge for many days now, especially since my physical exam, but so far I've been able to keep my mind separated from the vast pit of despair that is now consuming Sarah.

I am exhausted and feel sick to my stomach. There is no way out for any of us, and I know it will take a miracle from God to deliver us from our squalor. There have been too many accusations against me, and too many against the other women who share my cell. None of us are willing to accuse more women of witchcraft so that we might be set free, and we are paying that price.

It is high, indeed.

I struggle to my feet, feeling as if tiny needles are pricking my skin all over from being on the hard ground for so long.

"Sarah," I whisper, rubbing her shoulder. She flinches away from me and moans.

"Are you ill? Are you cold?"

She only sniffles and wraps her arms tighter about herself.

"Tell me about your family," I say. As much as we miss our children and families, speaking of them can help us keep our minds above the anguish.

It's a long moment before Sarah speaks. "Why do you care?" Her voice is rough and harsh.

I hesitate at the tone, but I am already awake and the other women are likely as well. In fact, I hear Rebecca whispering prayers to herself. The cell is dark, but the moon casts enough light through the tiny window above to illuminate our misery.

"I miss my family, too," I say, barely above a whisper. At least Sarah is no longer whimpering, but looking at me now. "I have nine children, eight of which I bore. Each of them more stubborn than the next." I have spoken of my children many times, and surely Sarah has overheard.

She blinks as me, and her breathing calms, so I continue, "There was a time that no one thought I'd marry, least of all my parents." I spread my arms. "If you can believe it, I used to once be fatter than our biggest cow."

Sarah smirks. "I don't believe you."

I smile. "Maybe not that fat, but I was nothing like my beautiful sister, Mary, who married well before I caught a man's eye."

"But you caught him good, it seems, with all those children," Sarah says, pulling herself to a sitting position.

"I suppose I got him good enough," I say. Her eyes are brighter now, more aware.

The baby stirs next to her, and we both watch the child.

"She's not eating," Sarah whispers so softly I almost don't catch what she's saying.

"Have you plenty of milk?" I ask.

"Enough for such a small thing," she says, but her voice is edged with fear. "This past morning, she spat up all that she ate. And then she refused my breast at noon-day and again tonight. But she's not fussy . . . is that unusual?"

I watch the baby sleep in the moonlight. She looks so peaceful. The dim light fades the dirt and grime, and if I didn't know better, the child could be any of ours, sleeping through the summer night. Her daughter, Dorothy, sleeps against the wall, her back to us. Her thin shoulders rise and fall with her child breaths.

Sarah's baby sighs in her sleep, a small sound like a kitten.

"She'll be hungry like nothing else in the morning," I declare.

A faint look of relief crosses Sarah's face.

The woman seems more settled now, more like the fierce independent woman that I've come to know. She doesn't let any of the other women close to her, but there is camaraderie between us nonetheless. We are all living in the same unfortunate circumstance, and we either eat together or starve together.

Our souls have become woven together, no matter our backgrounds.

As her baby sleeps and the other women around us relax in the quiet, Sarah says, "You may have noticed my husband never comes around."

I have noticed, but none of us have dared to ask about it.

"William accused me to save himself," she says, her voice quiet and heavy. "He told the court that I am an enemy to all good."

I have heard of this from time to time. Husbands and wives turn on each other in their panic and desperation. As long as you are doing the accusing, then you don't become the accused. I'm ready to voice my sympathy when she speaks again.

"He wants me dead, that's what," she says. "Everyone knows that the Bible says witches shall not be permitted to live. So it's quite a most convenient way to get rid of me."

I try not to stare at her, but my mind can't quite grasp it. "I thought you were accused by those girls."

"Yes, I was, in the beginning." Sarah pulls her thin legs up to her chest and wraps her arms around them. "No one in town liked me, you see—my husband and I had fallen on hard times. For most of our marriage, it's been that way, it seems. And the good Christians of Salem hate to see a destitute woman."

"Not very Christian like, then?"

Sarah's mouth moves into a half smile, or maybe it's a half grimace. "I thought prison would be the death of me, but that wasn't the worst part. It was when they accused my little Dorothy as well and forced her to confess."

I nod, thinking of my own children. Fortunately, none of them had to appear at court and testify. There's something to be said for a mother enduring the worst, but when her child has to endure the worst, the helplessness is crippling.

"Everyone hates each other in Salem," she whispers, and I lean forward to make sure I've heard right.

"I know there are those who take sides in your town," I say. "Some with the Putnams and some with the Porters because of the new church building. But surely that will die down over time."

Sarah is shaking her head. "Not until one side has driven the other out. The Putnams want their own church—so they can make the laws and collect the money. Everyone who supports the Porters wants things to remain as they are. We came to this country so we could have freedom. The Salem church will only be something that controls everything and everyone in the town."

She blows out a shaky breath, and I see this strong woman has been broken. "I'm a disgrace to the Putnams and their high and mighty kind," she continues. "How dare a beggar exist in their town? I remind them of the squalor they left behind, and they are afraid of me—afraid of what I represent. Afraid that they are only a few steps away from becoming like me." Sarah shifts forward, as if she doesn't want any of the sleeping women to overhear. "The Putnam family is behind most of the accusations."

A shiver runs across my skin.

"Think about it," she continues. "The twelve-year-old girl, Ann Putnam, has the power to imprison me. Who gave her that power?"

My mind goes to when I was first brought to court and faced the magistrates. The group of girls moaning and wailing was pitiful, frightening, and disturbing. The same teenaged girls accused me of appearing to them as an apparition, and then they sat through my court appearance and acted as if I was tormenting them.

Their names churn through my mind: Elizabeth Hubbard, Mercy Lewis, Mary Walcott, Ann Putnam, and more. It is astounding how many people agree I am a witch.

"They accused me, they did," Sarah continues, "of blaspheme against the church because I have no self-control or discipline. Because I must beg for my food and shelter means that I am evil." She coughs out a laugh. "This means that I scorn those girls who accused me. I scorn the Puritan way of life; therefore, I must have signed the devil's book."

My stomach tightens as I think of all Sarah has said. Not only are innocent women, men, and children in prison, but the very beliefs that are supposed to redeem us from oppression have now enslaved us. My mind is tired, and the darkness of the cell seems to close around me.

I lean against the cold wall as Sarah continues whispering. Her life has been hard; mine has been easy compared to hers. I do not know how she has endured so much, but I am certain of one thing as I watch her care for her two young children in the worst of conditions. Sarah Good is no witch.

CHAPTER 8

Salisbury

MEETING WAS CROWDED TODAY, and I knew it was from the breakout of an unknown rash. Whenever an illness reached our town, the less faithful became faithful again, seeking blessings and promises from the reverend.

He was in full form today, his black robe looked suitably stiff and his white collar freshly laundered and starched. I didn't have time to search for the Martins before my parents ushered me into our family pew to sit next to Mary and her husband, Thomas. Her family had spent the night at our farm. I had pleaded a headache the night before and gone to bed early to avoid Mary's incessant questioning and speculation. This morning, the children took over the household, giving us no time to talk.

It seemed Mary had read my mind, and she reached over and grasped my hand, then whispered, "Third behind us, right side."

My eyes widened, and she only smiled at her cleverness.

But as the opening hymn began, my gaze slid back to

where George sat. He sat straight and erect, singing his heart out. Next to him was his sister, and on her lap was a small girl, not even two yet. Her tiny arms were wrapped around Eve's neck, and her dark hair was pulled into two severe braids. I didn't see much of George in Hannah's features, so she must take after her mother. Hannah's large, soulful eyes looked at me, then moved to Mary's squirming children. As if George sensed being stared at, he turned his head and saw me. Our eyes locked for a second, and he smiled.

I looked down quickly at my hands, as if I had something very interesting to inspect. I felt my skin warm and a flush creep along my neck. When I dared to look over again, he was properly facing forward again. Hannah had been distracted by something else as well.

I didn't hear a word from the reverend for the next hour, or perhaps it was two. I mouthed the words to each song, but my voice had completely disappeared. Whatever was happening to me, I refused to look at the third row any longer, no matter how much my eyes tried to betray me.

"Come," Mary said, touching my arm and breaking me out of my stupor. "We're gathering to eat in the grove."

Half of the congregation had already filed out, and despite my resolve, my head turned to find George. He was nowhere to be seen, and relief shot through me. Perhaps he wouldn't stay for the afternoon session. And perhaps his family didn't know about the tradition of sharing food with our neighbors between sessions so we didn't have to travel back and forth.

But when I stepped into the grove, my luck ran thin. George was there with his daughter, holding her, while his sister sat some distance away, hovered over by women from the town. Several young women stood clustered around George, smiling at him, then ogling Hannah. George laughed at something someone said, and it sounded clear across the glade. A few disapproving glances were sent his way, but that didn't seem to deter him.

Even though we were no longer in the Meeting House, we were to behave properly the entire Sabbath day.

I stayed with my family and spoke to a few of my mother's friends, but that didn't prove to be much of a distraction because everyone wanted to talk about the new Martin family. If there was one thing about our community, it was that everyone knew everything about each other. And they were more than happy to talk about it.

"Goody Martin has been ill for a number of years," Widow Leeds said. "She's suffered greatly and she only has one brother to look after her." She lowered her voice. "I don't know how she deals with a young child in her home as well."

My mother put her hands on her hips. "We'll take good care of her as a neighbor. I've taken her some of my best tea leaves. She tells me they are already helping. Look, she's at Meeting today, isn't she?"

My gaze strayed from the conversation to see Anabel smiling up at George. The girl was so brazen; anyone from a mile away could guess her interest. George was smiling back, but just as I was watching them, he looked over at me.

I moved slightly, as if I was just turning, and focused back on Widow Leeds. "She is so thin," I said, without thinking. I didn't want to be involved with talking about the Martins, but I had to force myself to stop snatching peeks over at George.

Widow Leeds nodded, and my mother said, "She thinks Susannah is a dear."

Clasping her hands together, Widow Leeds said, "It is so very important for a girl to get along with her sister-in-law."

I stared at the woman. I didn't even dare look at my

mother, who surely wore one of her knowing smiles. I couldn't let this pass. I couldn't let this topic be discussed in other circles. So before I could bite my tongue, I said, "I am sure you are right, but it seems George has already been snapped up by Anabel. I couldn't be happier for both of them."

Mother gasped, and Widow Leeds did a half turn to inspect the blooming couple for herself. "Well . . ." It appeared that she was speechless.

"We should go find our benches so that we don't have to go in with the crowd," I said to my mother. She agreed, and we collected my father and Mary's family and made our way back to the Meeting House. I didn't pay attention to the Martins this time, for I kept my gaze rigidly forward.

When Meeting finished, I said good-bye to Mary and her husband and children, who climbed in their wagon and headed to Gloucester. I then followed my parents and Sarah and Ann to our wagon. They dawdled, speaking to some people, so I found myself approaching the wagon alone. George was standing near our wagon, as if waiting for someone, and I nearly turned around. Instead, I steeled myself and continued forward.

He tipped his hat, his amused eyes on me. "Good day, Susannah."

"Good day," I said, not sure which direction to go, since he was blocking me.

I made a move to go to the left, and he straightened. "Might I walk you home?"

I had to stare at him. His sister and daughter were nowhere in sight. Did he expect his sister to drive their wagon back by herself? Didn't he know how the town would speculate if we walked home together? My stomach both churned and flipped at the thought. But first, I couldn't let his dark gray eyes reel me in. I looked down at my folded hands. "I don't have time to walk today. I have so much to do once at home."

His reply was quick. "Not resting on the Sabbath?"

I lifted my eyes to his to see that he was teasing, not reprimanding. "Is Sabbath ever a day of true rest?"

His mouth quirked into a smile. "How do you define a true rest?"

"One in which I wouldn't have to get out of bed."

He laughed, and my face flushed.

"Until that day comes," he said, "I think a walk home from Meeting is in order. Surely it can't put your life on hold for too long."

I almost smiled back, but the nerves in my stomach had doubled. When I was around him, I was not myself. I didn't trust what I might say or do, and I certainly didn't trust what others might say either.

"What about your sister and your daughter?" This was the first I'd spoken of his daughter, but he didn't seem to mind.

"We rode with the reverend today. They have a way back."

I wavered, tempted. But seeing my parents approach out of the corner of my eye, my resolve strengthened. There would be endless questions if I allowed George to walk me home.

"I'm sorry, George, I must return with my family," I said. "Have a good Sabbath." I turned from him then to see my parents approaching.

My mother's gaze was bright on George, and he greeted them affably, but I detected disappointment in his voice. Which just made my heart flutter more. I wished he would hurry and court Anabel so that my life could get back to normal.

I didn't know my wishes had so much power until my family's wagon passed by George and Anabel. He was walking with *her*. I turned my gaze so I wouldn't be caught staring as we passed.

My eyes burned. What was wrong with me? Why did I care—wasn't this what I wanted? I exhaled carefully so as to not draw attention from my parents with a sigh. Seeing George turn to Anabel so quickly confirmed my doubts. He wasn't truly interested in me, and compared to Anabel, I was plain, short, and too round.

He had asked me first, but maybe that wasn't significant to him in the long line of girls he seemed to be acquiring. Of course, with Anabel at the top of the heap, the others girls wouldn't fight too much. They knew when they were beaten.

I closed my eyes for a few moments, letting whatever hope I might have had about George die within me. Admitting that I did have hope was hard enough; letting it go was even harder.

The Apparition of Susanna Martin of Amesbury did most grievously torment me during the time of her examination for if she did but look personally upon me she would strike me down or almost choke me and also the same day I saw the Apparition of Susanna Martin most grievously afflict the bodies of Mary Walcott, Mercy Lewis and Ann Putnam by pinching and almost choking them and several times since the Apparition of Susanna Martin has most grievously afflicted me by beating and pinching me and almost choking me to death, and that she believes the said Martin is a witch and that she is bewitched by her.

—Sarah Vibber, age 36

CHAPTER 9

Salem Jail

"SHE WON'T WAKE UP," Sarah Good whispers, nudging me awake.

My eyes fly open, and I'm momentarily disoriented. But I realize that it is Sarah who had nudged me and not some rat. I must have fallen asleep listening to Sarah's stories.

I turn to see Sarah bent over her infant, gently tapping her face. "Mercy," she says once, then twice, her voice growing louder.

"What are you doing?" I ask, moving into position to get a clear view. "Why are you trying to wake her up?" The sun has not yet risen, and for a short time, I was in a deep sleep, with or without rats.

"My breasts are engorged," Sarah says. "They haven't been this way since my milk first came in."

I pull Sarah's hands away from her baby. "Let the child sleep. You can let your milk down, and there will be plenty more when she's ready."

But Sarah is shaking her head, and tears pool in her eyes. "Something's not right, I tell you."

"Let me see the child," I say, and Sarah moves over. I kneel next to the sleeping infant and stroke her cheek. Her skin is cool to the touch. The night is warm, even in the cell. I reach for Sarah's hand and confirm that her skin is warm, as is mine, despite our deplorable condition.

A chill runs through me. I have borne and raised eight children, so how can I be so far off the mark? The child is certainly not with fever, but skin too cool doesn't bode well either.

"Wake Rebecca," I say. "Ask her to pray for the child."

Sarah's eyes meet mine, full of fear. Without another word to me, she scampers across the cell and wakes Rebecca.

Hands trembling, I lift the small child in my arms and place my ear to her chest. Her heart is beating, but as I move my cheek to just above her lips, her breath is very faint.

"Mercy," I say as I hear Rebecca praying, her voice growing louder.

Sarah is back at my side. "We must warm her," I tell Sarah.

All of the women are awake now in the cell and crowd around us. Elizabeth hands over a shawl and I bundle little Mercy, then hand her to Sarah's waiting arms. "We'll find help," I say, trying to reassure her.

The mother clutches the child to her chest, letting out a moan.

I climb to my feet and move to the cell bars. "Sir," I call out. It is early yet, and the rest of the prisoners are already grumbling at the intrusive noise we're making. "We need a physician!"

"Quiet," someone calls out.

Yet another says, "He'll not come, you know."

But I continue to call for help, ignoring the disgruntled words from those who are awake, until I hear the footsteps of the jailer approaching.

"It's the infant," I say. "She needs a physician."

The jailer shakes his head. "You've to pay before I'll fetch him, but I don't know if William Griggs will help a witch's spawn." He well knows that Sarah Good has no money, and no hope of family paying for anything in her behalf.

I look back at my cellmates and see the stricken looks on their faces. William Griggs is the physician who diagnosed the afflicted girls and told the girls they were under an evil hand. What are the chances of him coming here, to the cells, to help Mercy Good? Perhaps the Lord will prick his conscience for a helpless babe.

I know there is no money among us. My gaze lands on Sarah, who is cradling her infant, tears streaking her soiled cheeks. There's no use to send for her husband. He'll not pay either.

Sarah Wildes joins me at the bars and pleads as well. "Please," she says to the jailer. "Please fetch the physician. We'll find a way to pay." She looks at me, and I nod.

"We'll pay extra if you hurry," Elizabeth says from behind us.

We all know, the jailer included, that Elizabeth would be able to get the funds from her family.

The jailer hesitates, looking from me, then to Sarah and the baby on the ground. He leaves, and we all exhale with relief and hope. Now all we can do is wait. I cross to Sarah, who has revealed her breast to try to feed Mercy, but the baby will not latch on. Sarah is sobbing now, and my own tears start. I wrap an arm around the woman's shoulders. Where she might have once rejected my touch, she now leans into me.

"Curse them for sending me here," Sarah cries. "Curse them all for—"

"Hush," I say. We cannot know who is listening; we cannot be too careful. Desperation knows no bounds.

I don't take my eyes off the child. The moon has finished for the night, and dawn slowly dispels the dark corners of our cell. It seems a lifetime since the jailer left to send for the physician.

Finally, footsteps sound, and I release Sarah to scramble to the bars. It is the jailer, and he is alone. I hurry to the bars to speak. "Is the physician on his way?"

He looks to Sarah Good, then back to me. "No," he says quietly. "The physician is attending to another woman—one who he says isn't accused of witchcraft."

My heart stills, and my breath stops. "It's an infant," I rasp, my throat thick. "An innocent babe."

The jailer gives me a brief nod, and for a moment, I see the exhaustion in his eyes. I think of what his life must be like—his days and nights spent guarding prisoners. But I also see the deadness of his eyes—there is no hope there. If anyone could have persuaded the physician, he could have.

"Did you offer him extra pay?" Elizabeth asks.

I hold my breath. Perhaps the jailer forgot to mention that the women of the cell were willing to pay extra.

"He said no," the jailer reiterates. "No offer of extra money will change his mind."

Behind me, someone sobs. I guess it to be Sarah Good, but it could be any of the women. Sarah's tragedy is our tragedy. I don't even want to know how much this will cost us—not in money, but with the town thinking that a child died because it was imprisoned with witches.

My breath catches. The child will die. I know this now. Despite my earlier assurances to Sarah, without a physician and his medications, there is nothing a group of helpless prisoners can do. The child's life is in God's hands now.

I turn away from the jailer, regret shooting through me. I think of my own children and grandchildren, safe this night, alive, warm, clean, and strong. Yet I share a cell with a feeble babe who is close to taking her last breaths.

I think of what Sarah Good will miss out on with Mercy. Sarah won't be able to hold the child again as she whimpers in the middle of the night, or pat her head as an excited toddler, or even swat her backside when she's disobedient.

All will be lost now.

"Thank you," I say to the jailer. "Thank you for trying."

The jailer only nods and turns away. I cross to Sarah, my eyes smarting at the cruelness and lies that have brought us to this place. Setting one foot in front of the other, I move across the cell to join the other women. As Sarah rocks Mercy back and forth, I kneel next to Rebecca Nurse. It's all I can do to keep from collapsing and adding my prayers to hers.

God's will be done.

CHAPTER 10

Salisbury

"TAKE THIS CREAM TO Goody Martin," my mother asked me. It had been two weeks since I had turned down George for a walk.

The following Sabbath, he again walked home a girl, that time it was Constance. It seemed George changed girls as often as he changed socks, not that I knew how often he changed his socks.

I hesitated but knew that Goody Martin loved my mother's cream. And if there was anything I could do to put color in the ill woman's cheeks, I would. I took the pitcher from my mother's outstretched hand, knowing she had intentionally asked me and not Ann, who was working on a stitching sampler in the kitchen.

"And George Martin should have the new horseshoes ready," Mother added. "See if you can bring them back."

George had a nice collection of smithing tools, and he'd offered to reshod our horses. There was always some sort of trade going on between our families, and I could never keep track of what was going back and forth. I stayed as separated as possible because being around George made me remember that I'd always be the girl he laughed at.

My cheeks burning at my torrid thoughts, I walked along the lane. I wouldn't cross the fields today, even though it would cut my time in half. I noticed as I approached the Martin homestead that the wagon was gone. Perhaps George had gone into town. I knocked firmly on the front door and waited a moment, then let myself in.

It was as Goody Martin requested. She didn't have the energy to come to the door most days, so she'd asked my mother to enter after knocking.

"Goody Martin?" I called out as I swung open the door.

"Over here, dear."

She was in the front room, a quilt square on her lap. Her eyes were bright today, and she smiled as I walked in. Hannah played at her feet with a set of rag dolls. The young girl looked up at me, eyes wide. When I gave her a friendly smile, she looked back down at her dolls.

"What do you have there?" Goody Martin asked, her voice light.

"My mother's cream," I said, crossing the room.

"Your mother is a saint," she said. "Set it on the butcher block, and I'll take it to the cellar later."

"I can do that for you," I said, doubting she'd have energy later and not wanting it to spoil before George could do it.

She nodded. "Well, then, it's behind the house."

I left through the front door and walked around the house. The sound of metal striking metal came from the barn. I'd thought George wasn't here because the wagon was gone; he must have loaned it out. He seemed to be making good on the horseshoes. I lifted the cellar doors, then went down the short flight of stone steps into the coolness.

When I came back up, I walked over to the barn. Perhaps the horseshoes would be done soon, and I could visit with Goody Martin while waiting. I hesitated before entering the barn, unsure if I wanted to speak to George. But I told myself not to be silly and forced myself to walk inside.

George was bent over the fire kiln, pounding metal. The first thing I noticed was that he had his shirt off as he worked in the heat. The rhythmic pounding reverberated through my ears, and I wanted to cover them at the sound. But I couldn't move. I hadn't seen the bare backs of many men, but the ones I had seen didn't look like the muscled version of George's. It was plain he was not new to blacksmithing.

The muscles in his shoulders and arms bulged with each strike, sending a tremor through my heart.

The pounding stopped, and George adjusted the piece he was working on. I took a step back, intending to leave as quickly as possible, but as he started pounding again, I found myself remaining in one place.

Watching.

After a few moments, I realized I'd been holding my breath. Taking a much needed breath of air, I forced myself to leave the barn and walk back to the house. Bare torso or not, my opinion hadn't changed of George Martin. He was too finicky for my taste, and he'd made it plain that he preferred other types of women.

Crossing the yard, the sun seemed intensely hot—much hotter than before. So it was with gratitude that I stepped into the cool interior of the house to say good-bye to Goody Martin. I'd decided that my father could fetch the horseshoes another time . . . when they were ready.

"Have a seat, dear," Goody Martin said as soon as I entered.

I hesitated, then complied. I could spend a couple of minutes visiting, then leave without being too rude.

She folded her hands in her lap and smiled at me. "Tell me how you are doing."

Goody Martin had a way of making me feel like I was important, even worth paying attention to, but I honestly didn't know how I was doing. The thoughts running through my head were far from godly, and since they were about her brother, I didn't think it would be appropriate to share.

"I'm well," I said. "Are you making a quilt?"

Goody Martin's face twisted in what might have been confusion or pain. I was surprised at her reaction. She looked down at the piece of fabric in her hand as if she hadn't realized it was there.

"I . . . It's for George's baby, but he's gone now." Her hands trembled as she lifted the fabric square to her face and inhaled.

I stared in disbelief as the woman's eyes watered. "Goody Martin, are you all right?" I asked.

She said nothing, just closed her eyes and took several deep breaths. I didn't know what to do and wondered how my mother would help in this situation. I rose to my feet and clasped her hands. "Would you like to lie down for a moment? I can watch Hannah for you while you rest."

She nodded, her eyes still closed. Hannah hadn't moved from her spot on the floor nor seemed to notice anything amiss as she played with her dolls. I helped Goody Martin up, and we shuffled slowly to the back room. Tucking her in bed and pulling up her covers reminded me of taking care of a small child. Goody Martin looked small and fragile. I had not known she'd grieved so much over her brother's child. Perhaps she'd been close to his wife as well?

Goody Martin's breath was unusually shallow, and my stomach turned with worry. What if this wasn't normal? What if she'd taken a turn for the worse? I couldn't imagine explaining to George that I had been a witness but had done nothing but get her to bed.

I hurried back into the front room and scooped up Hannah, who surprisingly didn't protest. With her on my hip, I left the house to find George. No matter his state of dress, I had to let him know what happened. As I rounded the corner of the house, the barn came into view. George was leaning against the door, shirt still off, drinking water from a metal cup.

He straightened with a smile when he saw me coming toward him. Then, as if remembering his state of undress, he reached for a shirt that was hanging nearby and pulled it on. My step remained determined; this was no time for smiles.

Hannah reached out for her father, and George took her into his arms easily.

"Your sister seems to be ill," I told him. "We were visiting, and she suddenly became despondent."

George's expression turned from a lazy smile to concern. He carried Hannah with him toward the house. I followed after, not knowing what else to do, hoping I hadn't been the one to cause her episode.

"Eve," George said, heading straight for her room. He sat by her bed and took one of her hands in his.

"I can hold Hannah," I said, and he handed her over.

George leaned over his sister and touched her forehead, then her cheek. "What was she doing?"

I swallowed against my thick throat. "She was quilting, and I asked her about it. She said it was for your son . . ."

By the look of shock on his face, I decided to stop talking.

He looked back to his sister, then to me. "She talked about him?"

I nodded, unsure what else to say. I knew that his wife

had died in childbirth and the baby hadn't made it, but perhaps it lived a short time and Goody Martin became attached?

George patted his sister's cheek. "Eve, would you like some tea?"

The woman gave a faint nod, and George sat back, apparently satisfied.

"I can make it for her," I offered.

George gave me a grateful glance, and I hurried out of the room. I set Hannah down with her dolls again. It took only a moment to find the tea things, but by the time I returned to Goody Martin's bedroom, she was sound asleep.

George took the teacup from my hands and set it on the low table by the bed. Then he motioned for me to follow him. I was nervous as a mouse as I walked with him into the front room. At least he had a shirt on, but it was open at the neck, and I could smell the scent of his hard work.

"My wife, Hannah"—he glanced over at little Hannah—"she died in childbirth, as you know. The boy, we named him Christopher after my father, lived a few hours, then he was gone too. Eve took it very hard. I thought she'd show more interest in little Hannah—that my daughter would bring her comfort—but she's only recently paid attention to Hannah, and—"

"George," I said, putting a hand on his arm. "You don't have to tell me. I won't say anything, and you can keep your family's privacy."

George looked down at my hand on his arm, and I nearly pulled away in embarrassment. But he placed his hand on top of mine, and my breath hitched at his touch.

"I'd like to explain."

I nodded, vowing not to interrupt again.

"She thought that my wife and Christopher dying was a

curse from God. That He was unhappy with her because she never married or had children. Hannah and I had taken care of her, mostly Hannah, of course, while I took care of all the outside chores, along with my blacksmithing work. Eve and Hannah became the best of friends."

I couldn't stay silent. "Your sister is a good woman. God isn't punishing her—"

"I've tried to convince her of that, but she wouldn't listen." His gaze was filled with pain, and I wondered how long he'd had to keep his sorrow inside. "Our reverend was convinced that if she was a devout believer, then she'd become well. For a long time, she hid her sorrow. And she still does, but it's exhausting for her. I've heard her crying at night for my wife and Christopher—still, after all of these months."

His eyes had reddened, and my heart felt like it was being squeezed. Here was a man battling the same grief as his sister, yet he had to go on and provide for the family. He hadn't been able to grieve properly himself. I wanted to embrace him, but I daren't. I placed my other hand on top of his. He lowered his head, and we were only inches apart, only our hands touching.

"Her sorrow runs deep," I said, "but she is a righteous woman. She should not fret for her salvation."

George nodded, and I hoped that he agreed with me, but I wished I could do more. "Do you think it would help if I finished the quilt she started for your son?"

George looked at me for a long moment. "I can ask her."

"I'm happy to do it, if you think it would help. Maybe having it finished will help her bear the sorrow."

His gaze was tender as he studied me, and I felt my face heat. He was still practically undressed, at least for a Puritan man. And we were holding hands, standing close together.

I released him and stepped back. "I will come tomorrow to see what she has decided." Then I turned because I couldn't trust myself in this room any longer with George. Especially knowing he was courting other women, and that didn't include me.

George didn't follow me out, but I felt him watching me.

Some time about five years since, one of the sons of Susanna Martin Senior of Amesbury exchanged a cow of his with me for a cow which I bought of Mr. Wells the minister which cow he took from Mr. Wells his house. About a week after I went to the house of Susanna Martin to receive the cow of the young man her son. When I came to bring the cow home notwithstanding hamstringing of her and halting her she was so mad that we could scarce get her along, but she broke all the ropes fastened to her. We put the halter two or three times round a tree which she broke and ran away and when she came down to the Ferry we were forced to run up to our waists in water. She was so fierce but after much ado we got her into the boat, she was so tame as any creature whatsoever, and further this Deponent saith that Susanna Martin muttered and was unwilling this deponent should have the cow.

—John Atkinson, age 56

CHAPTER 11

SARAH'S MOURNFUL KEENING FILLS the cell, and it's as if my heart has been torn out of my chest. The child has taken her last breath. I do not know if a physician could have saved her, but it seems that God has other plans for the small soul. The child had not even been baptized yet. What will happen to her small soul?

The numbing presence of death is felt all the way to my bones. I move to the pitiful woman and wrap my arm around her shoulder as she rocks her silent child. My day of humiliating examinations seems a small thing now, of little significance. All of my children are alive and well and safe from prison.

The loss of a child to a mother can be felt all the way to the heavens. Surely God knows the grief; surely He will comfort us. But the comfort does not come, at least not now.

What trials are we meant to endure in this life? And how did the trials of regular life escalate to this horror? I wonder if there is so much a soul can endure before death seems the better option. For I look upon an innocent babe now, and she has escaped an earthly hell. Even if she had lived and her mother released, what would they have to look forward to? Sarah Good was ostracized by her Puritan neighbors long before the cell door closed upon her. Her own husband betrayed her.

And now it seems, she has lost what was left of her hope.

The other women join me in comforting Sarah. We hold hands in a circle, surrounding her and the child, and we bow our heads in prayer, speaking the words we have been told that no witch could ever utter.

"Our Father, which art in heaven,
hallowed be thy name;
thy kingdom come;
thy will be done,
in earth
as it is in heaven.
Give us this day our daily bread.
And forgive us our trespasses,
as we forgive them that trespass against us.
And lead us not into temptation;
but deliver us from evil.
For thine is the kingdom,
The power, and the glory,
for ever and ever.
Amen."

CHAPTER 12

Salisbury

"THANKS FOR COMING," GEORGE said as I stepped into his house.

"What did your sister decide?" I asked, breathless from my walk.

"She said yes, that she'd like you to work on the quilt." George shut the door behind me. "Come on back. She'd like to talk to you."

I followed him, trying to calm my heart. He looked freshly washed; the ends of his hair were still damp. He didn't smell of hard work like he had yesterday, but a scrubbed scent. His shirt was done up properly, though his cuffs were folded to his elbows. His skin had already tanned with the early summer sun.

"Dear Susannah," Goody Martin said as I stepped into her room. The sun came through the window, brightening the place up. Faint color stood in her cheeks, although it was far from the robust glow of a healthy woman. Little Hannah sat next to her aunt on the bed, clutching one of her dolls.

"Goody Martin, I'm glad to see you feeling better," I said. "Hello, Hannah."

The little girl merely blinked her large eyes at me.

George nodded toward the bed, and I sat next to Goody Martin. The woman reached out a thin hand, and I took it in mine. "George says you're to finish Christopher's quilt," she said.

"It would be an honor," I said, my voice cracking a bit.

She squeezed my hand. "Thank you. His eyes were blue, and I've run out of blue thread."

"My mother has every color imaginable. I'm sure I can match what you've already used," I said. George shuffled behind me, and I glanced up to see a soft smile on his face. Our gazes locked, and my heart skipped a beat. *Don't think about him now,* I commanded myself, and turned my attention back to his sister.

"Bless you, child," Goody Martin said. "I have spent many months trying to finish it, but each time I begin . . ." Her eyes watered.

I leaned over and kissed her cheek. "Don't fret about it now. I'll return it soon, and you can tell me what needs to be unpicked."

The woman smiled—a faint one, but a true one. "I'm not as nimble as I used to be, so I'm sure whatever your skill, you will out master mine." She raised a shaky hand. "There, on the bureau, you'll find the quilt pieces that I've started."

I rose and crossed the small room, standing close to George as I inspected the squares. About four of them were quilted; the rest had yet to be started. "I'll follow the pattern you've set," I said.

Goody Martin nodded. "Thank you again, dear." Her gaze slid to George. "Make sure you don't send our guest away without a jar of preserves."

"Yes, ma'am," George answered, amusement in his voice. He crossed to her and kissed her cheek. "Rest now, I'll return soon to check on you." He scooped up Hannah, who beamed at him, then nestled against his shoulder.

"Don't fuss over me, George," Goody Martin said. "You've your own work to do without worrying about your sister."

"I'll get Hannah down for a nap, and then I'll be back. There's not a thing you can do about that," he said with a laugh.

I smiled at the interchange. George was pretty good about bullying.

I gathered up the pieces and said good-bye. George grabbed a jar of preserves and handed it to me as he followed me outside.

Thanking him for the gift, I stopped at the door. "No need to walk me home. Your sister needs you."

His brow lifted. "She practically kicked me out. You heard her."

"Nevertheless, I'll manage," I said. "Besides, you've got to get Hannah down for a nap." I glanced at her. "She's a quiet child."

He shrugged. "She imitates her aunt and stays quiet. I'm sure that will change if I marry again, especially if there are more children."

I felt my pulse increase, so I changed the subject. "It shouldn't be too long before I can finish the quilt. I usually sew in the evenings anyway."

His gaze stayed on me. "Are you going to the annual celebration tomorrow night?"

I lifted a shoulder in a shrug. I might have been going if I was interested in dancing with any of the men from town. But there wasn't anyone I wished to encourage.

I was settling in at twenty-five and enjoying it as a single woman. I could come and go as I pleased and didn't have to worry about waking up in the middle of the night to feed a child.

George was still waiting for me to respond, an amused look on his face. Would he never stop laughing at me? "I hadn't planned on going," I said. "I'd rather work on the quilt for your sister."

He leaned against the doorframe, watching me. "Don't you like to dance?"

I flushed. I actually loved to dance. "There are a couple of men I'd rather not dance with. It encourages them, you see."

He looked very interested now. "Which men?"

"Oh, I don't want to say names." I paused. "Thank you for speaking to your sister for me. I should be going."

"Susannah," he said, his hand grasping my arm as I turned.

I stopped, but did not look at him.

"What if *I* asked you to dance?"

My heart thudded, and I dared look over at him. "I don't think you'll have a free dance to offer me. What, with all the tittering women, your head will be spinning before the night is through."

He considered for a moment, then said, "What if I did have a free dance?"

I stepped back from him, and his hand fell. "I guess we won't ever know, will we?" I opened the door and let myself through, my face reddening at his chuckling.

But I held my head high as I walked away from him, even though I could feel his eyes burning into my back. I didn't care if he laughed at me. If he wanted to invite me to a dance, it would be without any other women hanging on him, and it would be because his intentions were serious. I was not about to vie for any man's attentions, even if it was George Martin.

April 30, 1692, Salem Town: Jonathan Walcott and Thomas Putnam of Salem Village swore a complaint against Rev. George Burroughs of Wells, Maine; Lydia Dustin of Reading; Susanna Martin of Amesbury; Dorcas Hoar and Sarah Morrell of Beverly; and Philip English of Salem for tormenting Mary Walcott, Mercy Lewis, Abigail Williams, Ann Putnam Jr., Elizabeth Hubbard, and . . . Susanna Sheldon. Hathorne and Corwin issued warrants for all the suspects, sent for Burroughs from Eastward, and ordered that the rest be brought before them at Ingersoll's by ten o-clock the following Monday.

—excerpt from *The Salem Witch Trials*
by Marilynne K. Roach

CHAPTER 13

Salem Jail

THE DAYS PASS IN a stupor. And whatever we try, Sarah Good will not speak to us. We are left to pray and survive this place of hell moment by moment, hour by hour.

Elizabeth and I take turns forcing Sarah to eat a little each day. Her dead baby has been removed from the cell and given a pauper's burial—not even a marker with a name. None of us were allowed to attend. We have watched over little Dorothy as Sarah is too despondent to do so.

At night, I dream of George and our children, and in the day, during my waking moments, I imagine him visiting me. He is always on the other side of the bars. I wish my imagination would bring him inside the cell. Perhaps angels, or ghosts, do not like prison either, no matter how strong their love for the ones left behind.

Rebecca Nurse's family sends us bread and overripe tomatoes. She shares with all of us—just as we expect. As we sit together, gnawing on our bread and trying not to eat too fast, Sarah Wildes asks Elizabeth Howe of her life in Ipswich Farms.

"Your husband was blind, was he not?" Sarah Wildes says.

I am surprised at the frank question, but we have been confined together for so long, it's impossible for reservations to exist any longer.

Elizabeth doesn't seem bothered by the question. "He was blinded at age fifty," she says in a soft voice. "And I ran the farm after that. Our neighbors didn't care much for me anyway, so seeing me make decisions beyond a wife's duty only grated on them more."

"The Perleys?" Sarah Wildes asks. "Was it their daughter who had the fits?"

"Yes. Her name was Hannah." Elizabeth turns her remaining piece of bread over in her cracked and filthy hands. "The girl claimed I was pricking her with pins from afar. The doctors said that the child was under an evil hand." Elizabeth shoves the last of her bread in her mouth and chews for a moment.

From her corner, Sarah Good's eyes are open, watching us. Her bit of bread lays untouched next to her on the floor.

"It didn't take much else for one thing to lead to another," Elizabeth continues after she swallows, "and when Hannah died, the Perleys found a way to prevent me from going to church."

I shouldn't be shocked, but I feel a wave pass through me anyway.

"That was only the beginning, I'm afraid," Elizabeth said, sounding distant.

In the corner of the cell, Sarah Good picks up the bread at her feet and stuffs it into her mouth. We may not be able to get her to speak, but at least she won't starve.

Elizabeth nods to Rebecca, her cousin. "Rebecca knows this well, and so might all of you. We are no friends with the

Putnams. Years ago, my husband John asked the Putnams to produce deeds to the land they were claiming. Of course they couldn't."

Sarah Wildes scoffs. "The Putnams have hated my family for years." Sarah Wildes, although she is from Topsfield, knows the Putnams' wrath well.

Elizabeth pulls her thin knees up to her chest, as if to get comfortable, even though such a thing is impossible. "Not only did Thomas Putnam sign half of the formal complaints against accused witches, he also sits on the jury."

Rebecca adds, "Once the Putnams accused me, the Perleys jumped in and revitalized their accusations against Elizabeth."

With a sigh, Elizabeth looks toward the single window at the fading light. Another day has come and gone. Another day closer to our trials. "It seems the enemy list of the Putnams is long and extends to many towns."

"They think they are the law itself," Sarah Wildes says.

"And so they are." Elizabeth rests her chin on top of her knees. "We are in here, and the Putnams are out there."

As if on cue, a breeze cuts through the window, bringing with it the scent of green leaves and moist earth. I close my eyes for a moment, breathing it in, remembering my farm in Amesbury. What would it be like to touch the summer grass? To sift the rich warm soil through my fingers?

From the corner, Sarah Good shuffles to her feet. We all look over in surprise. She doesn't meet our gaze as she crosses to us and settles next to me in our haphazard circle. Her daughter, Dorothy, also rises from her place and follows her mother. She nestles against her mother like a small bird. Sarah Good doesn't even acknowledge Dorothy's presence, but she doesn't push the girl away either.

For a moment, none of us speak, and then Sarah Good speaks up, looking at Sarah Wildes. "What of the Putnams? How did you know them?"

Sarah Wildes draws her round face into a bitter scowl. "Does it truly matter? They accuse who they will."

We all nod at this, but Sarah Good is staring at Sarah Wildes with such interest—the only alertness she's shown in days—that Sarah Wildes continues, "I always made people nervous. Said I was too friendly of a person. Wore a silk scarf, as if that is any sort of crime. But I was brought to court for being too friendly with Thomas Wardell in 1649. And the year I married my husband, John, in 1663, I was brought to court again. It was no secret that my husband's first wife's sister hated me because John married me only six months after his wife died, who had borne him nine children. Her sister's name was Mary Goulds Reddington, and she started the first rumors. It will be no surprise to you that she's related to the Putnams."

I think of my father, who remarried Ursula. And of my own husband, who had been a widower before marrying me. "It's not so unusual for a man with children to want another wife quickly," I say.

"That may be, but there was already plenty of bad blood between John and his former wife's family," Sarah Wildes says. "In 1685, John had testified against his brother-in-law, Lt. Gould, when Lt. Gould complained about Royal Governor Edmond Andros. Gould was charged with treason, and there's been not a speck of forgiveness between the two."

"And I heard your son was the arresting constable," I say.

Sarah Good's eyes widen at this.

"No," Sarah Wildes says. "Marshal George Herrick arrested me, but my son, Ephraim, who is the constable at

Topsfield, arrested Deliverance Hobbs. Deliverance named me as a witch to get out of her own charges."

Sarah Good puffs out a disdainful breath of air. "If you lie and accuse another of witchcraft, you are exonerated. If you tell the truth, you are imprisoned."

"But that's not the worst," Sarah Wildes says with a nod. "My husband's daughter Sarah Bishop and her husband, Edward Bishop, were also arrested, along with his other daughter Phoebe."

We are all quiet at that. Sarah Good looks thoughtful, and I am grateful she isn't retreating again. There is only so much a heart and mind could handle. "God did say he would not give us more trials than we can bear."

My heart twists at the misquoting of scripture, one I've heard throughout my life. "No," I say softly. "The scripture in Corinthians doesn't say that."

Sarah Good peers at me, her brow pulled into confusion. I wish I could comfort her in this small thing, but it is better that we speak in truths.

"God says that he will not suffer us to be tempted above our capacity to resist," I say, feeling all eyes on me, although I am looking at my clasped hands.

"That's it, then?" Sarah Good says. "So we can be tried beyond our ability to endure?"

I raise my head to meet her gaze. Her blue eyes are intent on mine, filled with determination—which I'd rather see any day in place of despair. "Yes," I say. "I believe we can be tried beyond our endurance."

My voice is the only sound in the cell. But instead of the realization of my words making the women's heart shrink even smaller, a resoluteness passes through us. I reach for Sarah Good's hand, and she clasps mine tightly. Then she reaches for Sarah Wildes's hand, who reaches for Elizabeth's, who takes Rebecca's hand, until we have completed a circle.

"May God have mercy on our souls," Rebecca whispers as she bows her head and begins to pray.

CHAPTER 14

Salisbury

I DID NOT SEE George for the better part of the week while I worked on his sister's quilt. Mary and her family came into town for the dance and stayed at our home so they could attend market day as well. The next morning, she filled me in on the dance. I couldn't imagine Mary doing much dancing in her state; she had probably enjoyed the goodies more than anything.

I dared not ask about George directly but listened for any hints so I could dissect them later when I was alone.

"You should have come, Susannah," Mary said. "You know all the single men were there."

"You sound like Mother. I thought she'd faint dead away when I told her I wasn't going. She even planned to loan me her good shawl." We were sitting out on the porch, shelling a half bushel of peas between us. We would put up most of them, but save a dish for tonight's supper.

Mary placed a hand on mine to stop my shelling. "Why are you avoiding talk of marriage? You didn't used to."

I pulled my hand away and resumed shelling. "I'm tired of it, I guess. I mean, look at me . . . I'm as round as a barrel, and everyone knows that the pretty girls marry young. That leaves girls like me to marry the widowers." My eyes burned, but I plowed on. "I don't want to raise another woman's children the rest of my life. And I don't want to marry someone who I'll be serving hand and foot in a few years because he's too old to work anymore."

Mary stayed quiet, watching me.

The information wasn't anything new, but I hadn't put it all together before. I continued, "When I watch the younger women flirt with the men, it makes me tired. I don't flirt, Mary, and I'm not about to change now."

"Mr. Kimball asked about you."

I shrugged. Maybe a year ago, I might have been interested, but not since George moved into town. Of course, I couldn't let Mary know that. The men I might have once considered seemed lifeless and dull compared to George. "He's a nice man, but not for me."

"And Mr. Parris asked about you as well," Mary retorted. "You can't judge them so harshly, Susannah. We are all God's creatures, and we are not to judge each other."

"I'm not judging," I said, wondering if I was somehow sinning by refusing to be interested in a marriage partner. "I'm being selective." Yet, even as I said it, I knew it wasn't true. I planned to wait until all prospects were dried up, and I could be officially termed a spinster. It had worked for other women, and it could work for me.

"George Martin spoke to me as well."

My gaze snapped up, and Mary chuckled. "I thought that might get your attention."

"Not at all. I'm just wondering how his sister's doing. She had a bad spell the other week."

She gave a knowing nod. "Mother told me about the quilt you are finishing for her."

I hoped that the heat growing in my face wouldn't flame up. I hadn't told my mother the quilt was in memory of George's dead son, just that I was helping to finish it because of Goody Martin's poor health. "She's a good lady and a kind neighbor. Besides, I need all the blessings I can get, it seems."

"George is a handsome man, Susannah, and he's a hard worker. Devout, too."

I couldn't disagree, so I said what came to my mind first. "He's all that, I'm sure, but he can't be taken serious. He's a terrible flirt."

Mary laughed. "He said the same thing about you."

My hands stilled. "What?"

"It's true," Mary said, shaking her head with amusement. "He asked if you were actually staying home, and when I said you were, he said he thought you were doing it just to spite him."

I was quick to answer. "I did no such thing."

"He said you were a terrible tease and your way of flirting was to deny him any chance to spend time with you."

My mouth fell open. "If that's not the most backwards thing I ever heard. He just can't accept no for an answer."

Mary's smile widened. "Are you really telling him no?"

"Of course I am. I'm not interested in a man who enjoys having a dozen women dangling after him."

"He does have all the women worked up, but I don't think he's necessarily enjoying it."

"I've seen it with my own eyes," I said. "He has smiles for anyone who pays him the least attention."

"Yes, but he has eyes for only one of them."

"Anabel will be pleased."

Mary smacked my knee. "You're impossible."

I laughed, but inside I was fuming. George Martin didn't know who he was dealing with. He might have the courage to say those things to my sister, but he would regret every last word, I'd make sure of it.

[Magistrate] (to the afflicted girls): Do you know this Woman?

[Abigail Williams]: It is Goody Martin she hath hurt me often.

Others by fits were hindered from speaking. Elizabeth Hubbard said she hath not been hurt by her. John Indian said he hath not seen her Mercy Lewes pointed to her & fell into a little fit. Ann Putman threw her Glove in a fit at her. The examinant laught.

[Magistrate] (To Susanna Martin): What do you laugh at it?

[Martin]: Well I may at such folly.

[Magistrate]: Is this folly? The hurt of these persons.

[Martin]: I never hurt man woman or child.

[Mercy Lewes]: She hath hurt me a great many times, & pulls me down

Then Martin laughed again.

—Susannah Martin's Examination, May 2, 1692
Recorded by Cotton Mather

CHAPTER 15

Salem Jail

"BRIDGET BISHOP WAS HANGED today." The whisper echoes through the prison, and everyone stirs from where they are lying on the floor or leaning against a wall.

A man's voice comes from the next cell again, "Did you hear the news? The first hanging in Salem. Today, June 10, will not be forgotten." It is Roger Toothaker. His tone is thin and reedy like a cold spring wind tugging through newly planted trees. It's the middle of summer, yet the cold slips over me and runs deep into my bones.

I rise to my feet as do the other women in the cell. As one, we walk toward the metal bars to hear the news clearer.

Mr. Toothaker is a self-professed folk healer and claims to have killed a suspected witch with counter-magic. On the outside of this prison, he might have been my enemy. But as we are both on the same side of the bars, we are of like mind.

"Please, Mr. Toothaker," Rebecca Nurse says faintly, "tell us what happened."

I am surprised at Rebecca's request. She usually turns to prayer and God and doesn't worry herself about much else.

We know of Bridget because she's been in the cell next to us. I haven't specifically spoken to her, but she was said to have no moral character. She frequented taverns and dressed flamboyantly. She'd also been married three times. Her arguments with neighbors had been blamed for sick cattle and other animals. But her death sentence came when Abigail Williams, Ann Putnam, Mercy Lewis, Mary Walcott, and Elizabeth Hubbard all displayed seizures in the courtroom during Bridget's trial.

And now she's been executed by hanging.

The chill that had previously settled into my bones now seizes my heart.

"I've only heard rumors," Mr. Toothaker says.

Just then, the jailer comes down the corridor. His face is twisted with its usual wrinkles, although today, they are deeper than I remember. "You've heard the news, then?" the jailer says to no one in particular.

"Yes," Mr. Toothaker answers.

"They took her to the pasture north of here," the jailer says, startling us all with his frankness. "They loaded her into a cart. Guards surrounded the cart, and officers upon horses followed after."

His voice lowers, and a few of us shuffle closer so that we might hear. The prisoners in the other cell are quiet as well. "It was quite a procession, that I'll tell you," he continues, "especially when those accusing girls joined in."

Knowing that the young girls had been there makes my heart twist with new pain. Could they not even let the woman die in peace?

"They tied her hands behind her back, and her legs together, securing her dress closed," the jailer says, staring above the heads of the women in my cell. It's as if he was watching the execution again. "With the noose about her neck, the ladder which she stood upon was kicked out from beneath her. Death came slow to Bridget Bishop."

I turn away, squeezing my eyes shut. I imagine the convulsing body, the helplessness and panic that Bridget must have felt as she gasped her final breaths.

The jailer keeps talking, yet I barely comprehend. "Minister John Hale prayed for her condemned soul, but Mr. Thomas Maule shouted at him to stop. Said that Bridget Bishop covenanted with the devil and that was an unforgiveable sin—not one to be prayed over by a Christ-ian."

I feel my limbs weaken, and I cross the cell and lean against the wall. The summer sun pushes its warmth through the window opening above, yet it is deceptive. The sun might cast its golden web over land and trees and flowers, but in the prison, it only illuminates despair. One of our own has been hanged today. How many more will follow?

CHAPTER 16

Salisbury

IT WAS A FULL two days before I was able to finally speak my mind to George Martin. I'd finished the quilt, being driven like the devil running from the wind. The sooner the quilt was done, the sooner I could be finished with all things George. I didn't want to bring his sister into it, but if George was telling my own sister that I was a tease, who knew what he was saying to others?

The morning I delivered the quilt to his sister, I was determined to give George a good talking to. Fortunately, I found Eve in her usual place—sitting in her rocking chair, bundled in a quilt—and no George in sight. I didn't want her to witness what I meant to say to him.

"You are such a dear," Eve said softly, her eyes glowing as she inspected the quilt that I laid gently on her bed.

"I'm sure you could have stitched a finer line," I said. "And I'm happy to redo some parts if needed."

"Oh, no, this is beautiful." Eve ran her fingers along the squares, tracing their shapes. "My . . . Christopher would have loved it." Her voice trembled, and I hoped this wasn't the beginning of another episode. Fortunately, she looked up at me and smiled. "This brings me great peace."

"Wonderful," I breathed. And on impulse, I drew her into my arms and hugged her. Her return embrace felt fragile, but when I pulled away, a smile had filled her entire face.

"I'm so glad we're neighbors," I said impulsively. What was wrong with me? I was about to sever that neighborly bond with her brother.

After a few more minutes of visiting, I felt I could get away, and before I could change my mind, I walked toward the barn. I knew I had to make it quick. The quicker I was on my way home, the quicker I could reclaim Susannah North.

George was mucking out the horse stalls when I entered the barn. It was just as well, I didn't want to be anywhere near him, and the smell of the muck would excuse my distance. He turned when I walked in, and his face split into a grin.

"Your sister has her quilt now," I said.

His eyes appraised me, and I realized I'd worn one of my better dresses, unintentionally, of course. "Thank you for that, Susannah. You don't know what it means."

"I have an idea. She thanked me plenty, and I was pleased to help her." I took a deep breath. "I've one more thing to say about what you told my sister at the annual celebration."

He set his rake against the stall and took a couple of steps toward me.

Before he could get too close, I said, "I'd rather you not converse with her, or anyone else, about things concerning me."

His gaze was intent on me as he continued walking

toward me, but I wouldn't be swayed from what I'd come to say.

"I'm not a flirt, and I haven't been teasing you," I continued, feeling my face heat despite my desire to remain perfectly calm.

George said nothing but stopped at the water pump and washed his hands beneath the flow. Then he scrubbed his face and neck with water until the ends of his hair were dripping wet. He used a piece of cloth hanging near the pump to dry his face and hands.

When he could hear me again properly, I said, "Everything I've said—about not wanting to walk home with you or otherwise—has been the truth. If you choose to make fun of my wishes and not honor my desires, that's your concern."

His gaze was back on me as he walked closer, and with him nearer, I could see that his eyes were clear today—light gray.

I took a couple of steps toward the door. I didn't like how he'd reduced the distance between us. "So I'd appreciate it if you'd take a woman at her word and not turn things around."

George was standing in front of me now, his head tilted as he studied me. Perhaps he was taking me seriously after all. "I think what you need is a good kissing," he said.

I stared at him, my heart nearly in my throat, throbbing and making it hard to breathe. "A *kissing*? Who do you think you are, George Martin?"

"You know who I am, and you know what I mean." One of his hands stole to my waist, and I felt the warmth of his palm through my dress, all the way to my skin.

Somehow, I managed to speak. "George, you don't have permission to touch me."

His gaze locked with mine, and for a moment it was like staring into the depths of the ocean, and I was slowly rocking with the swells.

His hand dropped and took the warmth with it. Disappointment shone in his eyes as he straightened and stepped back. He lifted both of his hands, fingers spread wide in innocence. "I'm here to obey you. Just as you requested."

I watched his lips speak the words, but I didn't hear what he said. All I could think about was how his mouth might feel on mine and what it would be like if his hands truly possessed me. I'd watched him blacksmithing, working in the fields, repairing wagons, and helping my father more times than I could count. Each time his hands were working, muscled and efficient.

My breathing quickened, and I felt as if I'd ignite with desire so raw that it surprised even me. Before he lowered his arms and could put more distance between us, I grabbed his hands and pulled him toward me.

His eyes flashed in question, and I wanted to laugh. I'd finally done something even George couldn't misinterpret. But I wasn't finished. I reached for his shoulders and lifted up on my toes.

"Show me how this kissing is done, then," I said in a low voice.

He stared at me for a second until I went bright red. A slow grin parted his mouth, and his hands drew me against him.

Was it possible to melt without any sun at all?

He lowered his head until his lips touched mine. I held my breath, wondering what was going to happen next. Bits of fire seemed to be shooting through my entire body. He backed me up against the wall, and I gripped the tops of his shoulders as his mouth moved against mine. I hadn't any kissing experience, but it appeared George knew what he was doing, of course, on account of his previous marriage, so I imitated him until we seemed to blend in perfect unison.

His hands shifted to my waist, and he trapped me against the wall until I felt like I was in a cocoon between his body and the barn wood.

"Susannah," he said, as he broke from our kissing. "You make me crazy." His breath was hot on my lips, and I opened my eyes, feeling like I was coming out of a deep sleep.

His face was close enough that I could see the storm in his eyes; the intensity made my breath catch. He slowly moved his hands up my sides and to my shoulders, then he cradled my face. George's lips brushed mine, again and again, and it was like a taste of something sweet and spicy at the same time. His light kisses only made me want more.

I threaded my fingers through his hair, dragging him closer, ensnaring him into deepening his kisses. When his tongue touched mine, my body shuddered. It was a new kind of crazy.

"Susannah . . ." he said, breaking away again.

"I know, I make you crazy," I whispered.

He pressed his mouth on my jaw, then trailed kisses down my neck. I leaned my head back against the wall, exhaling. Was it proper to enjoy kissing this much? One of his hands moved to the small of my back while his other hand rested on my shoulder as he kissed the hollow of my neck.

I arched against him with a moan. "Now *you're* making me crazy."

"Good," he said, his hand sliding from my shoulder down to my breast.

I gasped. "George!"

He lifted his hand. "Sorry," he said.

I didn't want him to stop, though I knew that we had to stop. I was sure I had just committed at least a dozen sins—all of which would be hard to repent of because I didn't regret any of them.

Besides, I was still mad at him, and just because he was kissing me didn't mean that I forgave him. His mouth was back on mine, and I told myself I'd let it go on a little longer, then we'd have to return to reality.

"George," I said, in between kissing him. "Don't you have work to get back to?"

"Yes," he murmured. "But it can wait."

He pulled me tight against him, breathing in my ear, and I squirmed at the moist warmth, but he didn't let me escape. It took us both a moment to catch our breaths.

"So this was your best kissing?" I asked.

He lifted his head, his eyes the color of a cloudy sky. "It's just a sample."

I laughed. "George, you're the most arrogant man I've ever met."

"Or kissed?" His eyes held mine.

"You're the only man I've kissed."

He stared at me, one hand moving behind my neck and threading into my hair. "I find that hard to believe."

"Believe as you will, George Martin, but I'm speaking the truth."

He dipped his head, his face less than an inch from mine. "Then I'm honored, Susannah North."

CHAPTER 17

Salisbury

MY ENTIRE BODY WAS on fire, and I wouldn't be surprised if my feet didn't touch the ground as I walked back home after kissing George in the barn. He had insisted on walking with me, but when he tried to hold my hand, I'd refused.

As we walked side by side toward my home, I wasn't sure what had happened between us, but I didn't want him to make a public spectacle, even if we were only crossing the fields. What did our kiss mean? What did George mean by it? What did I mean by it? And if he held my hand—touched me—who could say that I wouldn't try to kiss him again?

I knew girls who'd kissed a whole lot of men before marrying. Some even became pregnant on purpose to hurry up the marriage proposal. Such thoughts sent heat through my face. I had never considered the marriage bed much more than a marital duty, but after the way George had kissed me, it might be far more interesting than I'd first considered.

George's hand brushed mine, and I nearly threw my

arms around his neck. Instead, I looked at him. "You aren't a very good listener." Looking into his eyes turned out to be a mistake. Their intensity pierced my heart.

"Have some compassion on me," he said. "If I had my way, we'd still be in the barn."

I bit my lip and looked down. His arm bumped mine, and I sidestepped away.

He let out a groan and said, "I'm sorry, I won't do it again. Come back here."

I shook my head. We were nearly to my yard. I stopped and turned, keeping a safe distance. "Thank you for walking me home." I stepped away from him, and he grabbed my arm.

I looked down at his hand on me. He let go, but stood close enough that I could practically feel him.

"When can I see you again?" he asked.

I gazed into his gray eyes. Did he really mean it? Was I more than just another woman dangling after him? "Well, we're neighbors, George, so I imagine it won't be long."

He chuckled, and I took the opportunity to escape. I had a lot to think about and to wonder about. The last thing I needed was my mother questioning where I'd been for so long.

I didn't see George until the next Sabbath. My family's assigned bench was several rows in front of his, so I didn't have the problem of trying to avoid his eye. During the meal break, he was surrounded by the usual group of women, and my heart died a little bit. But what did I expect? Perhaps he'd kissed each of them. I kept my distance and, even though I wanted to scream and throw something—most specifically at George—I remained calm.

Back in the second Meeting session, I took my usual place by my family, but then someone sat next to me. There wasn't much room left on the bench, so the fit was tight. I inhaled sharply as I realized it was George.

Did he not know how people would speculate? All of those women he'd been flirting with would see it as a slight against them. Or perhaps they'd think it was because we were neighbors—like we were brother and sister or something. Besides, our family had this bench assigned to us for as long as I could remember.

I tried to relax and tell myself George sitting by me wasn't anything to pay attention to. Although my parents had now noticed and glanced over a couple of times.

I wanted to question George, ask him what he was doing, and ask why he wasn't sitting by his sister and daughter. Perhaps they'd run out of room on their bench. I released a soft sigh. That was it. He could sit by me because I was a neighbor, but he couldn't sit by one of the other women because *that* would mean something.

I kept my hands tightly folded on my lap and my elbows drawn in as much as possible, but our arms and shoulders still brushed against each other at any little movement. We stood to sing, and George didn't give me any space. In fact, I was more aware of him than ever. His hand brushed against mine as he sang, his voice clear and strong. And then before I realized what he was doing, his fingers slid through mine.

"George!" I whispered as loud as I dared, tugging my hand away. He just stared straight ahead with a smile on his face.

My face heated, and I hoped that the reverend, and my parents, wouldn't notice.

When Meeting ended, he greeted my parents, said nothing to me, and slipped away. After his attempted hand-holding, I had at least expected him to ask to walk me home. I wouldn't let myself watch him walk away, or try to see whomever he talked to next. The fact was, I wanted him to walk me home, and I wanted to make the other women envious. At least for a short time.

And I was sure that was a coveting sin.

As we rode home in the wagon, I removed my bonnet, much to my mother's chagrin. But there was no one around, and my face had already started to freckle with the summer sun. What were a few more freckles? Plus, the sun on my face helped me see things more clearly.

I decided that George Martin was just a flirt, and it would eventually get him in trouble. He'd go kissing some young woman, and her father would find out and force a marriage. Or worse, he'd take it too far, and then there would be no chance of backing out of things. Perhaps that was the way of a man who'd been married before. And because of that, it was wise he married sooner than later. I was just one of his flirts. It felt nice, I admitted, and I was glad my first kiss had been amazing. At least I'd always have that if I lived as a spinster, or ended up marrying someone with cold, fish lips. I could think fondly back on George.

My face heated involuntarily, and I was glad my parents were focused on the road. Kissing George had been unlike anything I'd expected, and when I couldn't crowd out my thoughts with other concerns, it was all I thought about. But that would change with time. Each morning was a new day, and George would eventually latch himself onto some woman—forced or not.

In the meantime, I'd keep my distance and let things take their course. I'd just have to be careful with Mary; she could read me too well. I wouldn't let her know that my heart was on the verge of breaking because whichever girl George ended up with was sure to be a lucky wife.

"Can you take some cream to Goody Martin?" Mother

asked, pulling me from my stupor. We'd just arrived in our yard, and my father had climbed down from the wagon, extending his hand to me.

I took my father's hand, climbed down, and answered my mother, "Could it wait? I've a headache."

"You shouldn't have taken off your bonnet," my mother said. "I'll go over myself. I've been meaning to visit."

I went into the house and back to my room. It was nice to have it to myself. When Mary lived at home, I would have never been able to escape her chatter and think on something so complicated as George Martin.

[Mary Walcott]: This woman hath hurt me a great many times.

Susan Sheldon also accused her of afflicting her.

[Magistrate] (To Martin): What do you say to this?

[Martin]: I have no hand in Witchcraft.

[Magistrate]: What did you do? Did not you give your consent?

[Martin]: No, never in my life.

[Magistrate]: What ails this people?

[Martin]: I do not know.

[Magistrate]: But w't do you think?

[Martin]: I do not desire to spend my judgm't upon it.

[Magistrate]: Do not you think they are Bewitcht?

[Martin]: No. I do not think they are.

[Magistrate]: Tell me your thoughts about them.

[Martin]: Why my thoughts are my own, when they are in, but when they are out they are anothers.

—Susannah Martin's Examination, May 2, 1692
Recorded by Cotton Mather

CHAPTER 18

Salem Jail

THE DEEP VOICE FLOATS over me, barely penetrating my dreams of a better place, of a previous time.

"Goody Martin," the voice says again, and I open my eyes to find the cell bathed in the summer twilight. It's a few days after Bridget Bishop's hanging, and we've done little more than sleep the days and nights.

The filth of five women and a small child surround me, and I blink my eyes open, trying to moisten the dryness.

"Your family is here to visit," the voice again. It's the jailer. I recognize it now. And as my eyes focus, I see a small army of people surrounding him.

Three of my children stand there with their spouses. Richard, John, and Esther. I wish I would have known, but what would I have done? There is no place to wash, I have no change of clothing, and my fatigue is never-ending.

Still, I move to my side, then rise to my feet. The jailer steps back, allowing my family to crowd the bars, while he still keeps an eye on them. Exhaling, I steady myself. It always takes a moment or two to adjust to standing. I refuse to recognize their looks of horror and pity. I've long since accepted my living conditions.

Shuffling over to the metal bars, I push my hands through the openings so that I might touch these dear ones of mine. There is no hesitation in their embraces, but I can't forget the widening of their eyes as they take in the other occupants and surely smell the fetid air.

"Mother," Richard says, and the sound of his voice brings tears hot and fast. It is so much like his father's. If I didn't see Richard standing before me, I might have guessed George was speaking to me. "We've brought you food," he continues, stepping back slightly from the cell and opening a basket that his wife, Mary, has carried.

Her dark eyes flutter down as she pulls out a loaf of bread.

I can smell it from where I stand, even though it surely can't be fresh. The journey from Amesbury would have taken most of the day.

Behind me, the women awake and stir. They can smell the bread, too. I know they will not intrude on this private moment, though. We have respected each other in that way. They also know that when my family leaves, the food will be divided equally among us. It has been that way since I can remember.

"Thank you." My voice shakes with emotion, and I reach again for Richard. He grasps my hands and looks deep into my eyes.

"You are ill."

"I am as well as can be expected." I tilt my head as if to indicate the other women in the cell. "We help each other and share our food. We are better off than most because of the food you have paid for." Suddenly, I can't speak for a moment.

Esther steps forward, her husband, Henry, behind her. "Mother," she says, "I've finished the quilt and brought it for you." She kisses my cheek, followed by Henry. I am sure they can barely catch their breaths, but the affection is cherished.

I let out a laugh—my first in I don't know how long—and grasp the soft cotton quilt Esther hands through the bars. I bring it up to my face and inhale. A dozen memories clash inside me as I remember the hours I spent quilting and sewing, the time I spent teaching my daughters, Esther, Abigail, and Hannah, how to piece patterns and sew them together.

My frustration over this quilt pattern that I started before my arrest seems so futile now. If I could be released from prison, I'd never complain about a complicated pattern, or much else.

John's dear face comes into view, and I reach through the bars to grasp his hand.

"What can we bring you that won't be taken before it reaches you?" he asks.

So it must be true—the goods the family members send to the prisoners don't always make it through.

"We are in need of food and drink, always." I say this in a low voice because the jailer still stands close by. "Sarah Good's child died a few days ago, and—" My voice cuts off as I think of the innocent babe and the fate of Bridget Bishop. I cannot bear to think of it now, with me being on one side of the prison bars and my children on the other.

"We heard about Goody Bishop," John says. He tightens his grip on my hand, and although he doesn't say it, I know this is why my children have come today, despite my pleas for them to stay away from the prison.

On the day that constable Orlando Bagley, my former childhood friend, arrived with a court order of accusation issued by Jonathan Walcott and Thomas Putnam of Salem Village—a place twenty miles from my home in Amesbury—I had not imagined the proceedings would get this far. That I would be in prison more than a month, that I would stand naked before a jury, that I would live in a cell filled with innocent women, that a woman such as Bridget Bishop would be hanged for nothing more than conjecture.

I reach up and stroke John's face and look into his gray eyes—the same color of my George's. "Pray for me," I say simply. We need food, drink, beds, clothing, a physician, but who am I to dictate to God my fate?

My children crowd around, embracing me, touching my hand, kissing my cheek, loving me. It is the sweetest and most bitter experience of my seventy-one years on earth.

When my children leave, I curl up on the ground as the night shadows spread across the prison floor. The quilt that Esther brought is soft around me, and it feels like a bit of heaven. My stomach is full from the food brought by my family. My cellmates eat well too, but I need no thanks from them. The new hope in their eyes is gratitude enough.

Even little Dorothy climbs onto my lap and gives me a hug.

Seeing my family is a blessing I hadn't expected, and one I will be forever grateful for. And with their departure, I realize something else as well. My family has grown. It now includes Sarah Good, Dorothy Good, Rebecca Nurse, Elizabeth Howe, and Sarah Wildes.

CHAPTER 19

Salisbury

GEORGE STOPPED BY THE house twice during the next week, but I managed to avoid him, once with pretending a nap, the other by escaping out the back door so my mother couldn't find me. I don't know why I didn't want to talk to him. Maybe because I didn't trust myself not to kiss him again— or not to want to be kissed by him. And I wasn't about to become one of his *numbers*. Even though he'd tried to hold my hand in Meeting, I saw it as nothing more than one of his brazen acts. He probably laughed later about it.

On Saturday, my father commissioned George to refurbish our wagon with the new steel parts my father had ordered. George dragged the kiln from our barn and set it up right in the front yard. It was hard not to notice him as he bent over the heat, pounding out metal.

I was in the kitchen, helping my mother with supper preparations and trying not to steal glances out the front window, when my father came inside. "That boy has blacksmithing talent, yes, he does."

From what I saw, I agreed. But most farmer families stayed in the farming business. Blacksmithing skills just meant they didn't have to hire out that job.

My father continued, "He cut in half the time I would have spent on working the metal. He's nearly finished, and it's not even suppertime."

"He's a good lad to be helping this way," my mother said. "It would have cost us a fortune to have ole Parker do it. What are we trading for his work?"

My father took off his hat and scratched his sweaty forehead. "He won't tell me yet. Says he'll think of something fair."

For some reason, my heart thudded. I thought of what George might suggest. Maybe the loan of our horse, or a pint of my mother's cream for a week, or a couple of our chickens. With my parents talking, I stole another glance out the window. George was taking a long drink from a cup, his profile to me. He'd kept his shirt on, but it was practically soaked through with perspiration.

"You should take him some lemon-ice," my mother said, jolting me from my gazing. "It's exceptionally hot today."

I turned away from the window, hoping my face wouldn't go red. I gave a small nod, and went to prepare the refreshment. The ice was kept in our underground cellar, but wouldn't be ice much longer, not with a hot day like this. Outside, I could clearly hear George's pounding, and I hurried to the cellar, not letting myself dawdle and catch another look at him. I chipped off plenty of ice to make lemon-ice for everyone and then returned to the kitchen. My mother kept cut lemons in a preserved jar so that we'd have them several months longer than the twice-yearly delivery from the south.

I added the lemon and ice together, then a bit of sugar. My father took his and sat on the porch, leaving me to walk out to George, cup in hand.

He was hammering one of the wheel bands into place when I walked up. He straightened and wiped his forehead with the back of his hand when he saw me. His scent was strong from working and sweating, but it wasn't repulsive. It reminded me that he was a hard-working man.

Go easy, I told myself. "I brought you something cold. The day is hotter than expected."

George gave me a half smile, and his eyes shifted away as he took the cup from me. I'd expected him to grin or wink, or make some flirtatious comment. But he was quiet. Maybe he'd realized that his teasing had to end. Maybe he'd been courting one of the other women seriously at last.

He ate several chunks of ice. I took a step back, ready to turn, when he said, "I thought you moved to another county."

"Moved?" I turned to face him. "Why would I move?" He must be entering a new level of teasing, but the expression on his face was serious.

He lifted the hem of his untucked shirt and wiped the sides of his face, not even realizing that he was giving me a full view of his hardened stomach—or maybe he did realize it. "I came by twice, Susannah, and I know you were home. Why are you avoiding me?"

"I'm not avoiding you," I said, folding my arms over my chest and trying to keep my voice low. My father was still on the porch, although it looked like he was starting to doze.

"Oh, that's good to know. I figured either you were avoiding me, or you'd moved."

I held his gaze, which was still so serious. I didn't know how to react to this new George—this sober man. It was easier when he was laughing at everything and I could be annoyed by it.

"I have a lot to do, seeing how I'm the only daughter at home and my father's back ails him. My mother's not getting younger, either." I took another step away. "If you'd like more, let me know."

He gave me a nod, his mouth straight and firm, then said, "Mighty obliged."

I walked away, feeling huffy. What? Now we were fighting? He didn't own me, and I didn't owe him anything. Yes, I had been avoiding him, but I had been clever about it, hadn't I? If he was so bothered, then maybe he should stop by another woman's house, and who was to say he wasn't doing that already? He just wasn't used to be being put in his place. The other fawning women were making it too easy for him.

It didn't matter, I decided. At least now he knew where he stood, just like I knew where I stood with him. Back inside the house, I gave the dishes an extra good scrubbing. It was nice to focus on housework, and even my mother seemed impressed. That was worth something, wasn't it?

CHAPTER 20

Salisbury

SABBATH MEETING CAME AND went, and I stuck to my resolve of completely ignoring George Martin. I caught his gaze on me exactly two times, but otherwise, he was very engaged in conversations with Anabel or Constance. I didn't care who was who, only that I was finally being left alone.

My parents didn't notice anything was amiss, but I wasn't so fortunate with my sister. During her next market visit to town, she came to Meeting with us. And I told her that he and I had words, and I'd made it clear that I wasn't at his beck and call. "Look at him," I told her during the meal break. "He's making a fool out of every woman. What will Anabel tell her grandchildren? 'George had to get all of his flirting out of his system before settling down with me'? Or maybe it will be Constance."

Mary blinked her pretty eyes at me. "You're being thick, Susannah. He keeps looking over here, and I'll bet he's trying to get your attention."

"If he wants my attention so badly, he knows where to find me."

Mary arched her brows and lowered her voice. "Hiding in the cellar?"

"I didn't hide in the *cellar*." I'd merely gone to the barn to see if anything needed to be cleaned out.

She laughed. "Close enough."

Following the final Sabbath session, I'd just settled into the wagon when George approached my father. I kept my gaze forward as if I suddenly found the landscape very interesting. For once, I was grateful that my bonnet concealed the sides of my face, because what George told my father made me hotter than the mid-June sun.

"Mr. North," George started, "I've decided what I'd like to trade for fixing your wagon."

"Anything, son, you know I owe you," my father said.

"I'd like to walk Susannah home today."

My chest tightened, and it felt like the blood had drained from my body. Of all the nerve! Tongues would wag for sure now. Anabel and Constance would sneer at me. It might be all right for them to have some friendly competition over George Martin, but not with a third person in the mix, especially someone as plain as me.

"That's hardly a return of a favor," my father said. "I'm sure Susannah would be happy to walk with you, but there must be something more we can do for you. Maybe my wife can help your sister with some preserving this week."

"I'm sure my sister would be obliged," George said. "But that would be separate from this trade. Susannah walking home with me is a much bigger trade than you might at first imagine."

I could feel my father looking at me, and my mother had just arrived, certainly hearing the last part of the conversation.

There was no way out of it without being seen as a

toddler throwing a tantrum. Keeping my expression neutral, I scooted across the wagon bench toward the men. George stepped ahead of my father and held out his hand. Another defeat. I placed my hand in his and allowed him to help me down, while ignoring the warmth that shot through me at his touch.

"It is a nice day for a walk," I said in a too-bright voice. "Would you like to join us, Mother?"

"I'm tired after such a long week," Mother said. She glanced at my father with a small smile.

"What about your sister? Is she up to walking? Or Hannah? She'd certainly like to see the flowers and birds along the way," I said, turning to George, but not quite meeting his eyes.

"They've already left with the reverend and his wife."

I was stuck. My father and mother climbed into the wagon, and my father wasted no time in slapping the horse's reins and moving the wagon forward.

I stared after them for a second, partly in stunned disbelief, and partly because I didn't have the courage to look at George. I thought George was mad at me; maybe he meant to argue with me the whole way back to our homes. I set out, determined to get this walk over with. My strides were significantly shorter than George's so he had no trouble catching up with me and keeping pace.

We didn't talk for several moments, and at first I was content to let the whole way pass without a word, but then it started to bother me. What was George thinking about? And why did he want to walk home with me if he had nothing to say? Was it just to torture me? Because he knew I'd hate it?

But I didn't really hate it, and my heart was racing at the fact that he'd trade a day of grueling work just to coerce me into walking with him.

Although the sun was about an hour from setting, it was still quite hot, and without the wind that the wagon provided, my bonnet didn't keep me too cool. So I veered off the road and walked near the groups of trees, catching shade where I could. George stayed by my side, and when a wagon rumbled past, we both waved. It was the Ingersoll family and their three young boys. By the next morning, I was sure that word would get out who George was walking home *today*.

A second wagon went by, and I knew it would be the last one passing this way. That meant only silence stretched between us and the final half mile home. The longer we didn't talk, the more awkward it seemed to say anything. I imagined George spending each Sabbath walking a different woman home, maybe for years to come, and the town finally giving up on George getting hitched to anyone. I laughed at the thought, but hadn't realized I'd laughed out loud until George said, "What's funny?"

I looked over at him, feeling sheepish. He did look nice in his Sabbath finery; his dark blue coat made his eyes look more blue than gray, and his shirt underneath was snowy white. Unlike the shirt that I'd last seen him in. I decided I enjoyed both of his looks equally, which of course made me blush for no reason.

George's eyebrow quirked as he watched me. I looked forward again and said, "I was just thinking . . . Well, I don't know how to say it without offending you."

He slowed his step and touched my arm. "Will you tell me if I promise not to be offended?"

I stopped too, facing him. "All right." I took a deep breath. "With all of the women you seem to enjoy flirting with, I thought that perhaps it might be ages before you settle down. In fact, you might be quite an old man with a significant limp and only half your teeth before you choose your bride. And that would mean there will be many, many Sabbaths when the townspeople pass by in their wagons and see you walking a woman home."

George stared at me for a second, speechless. Was he mad? Offended after all?

He grasped my hand, and before I could pull away with indignation, he tugged me deeper into the trees until, even if a wagon did pass along the road, we wouldn't be spotted.

He stopped and released my hand. For that I was grateful because I didn't think I could endure much more touching by him. But then he raised his hands to my chin and untied my bonnet ribbons. He lifted the bonnet and tossed it to the grass.

"What are you doing?"

"Cooling you off," he said.

"I'm perfectly fine managing my own body temperature."

The amusement was back in his eyes, and I realized I had missed his teasing. I didn't care for the serious-George quite as much as I thought I would.

Then he stepped to the side of me and pulled out the pins from my braided bun.

"George," I protested, but it was in a weak whisper.

His fingertips brushed the back of my neck as he undid the braid. My body quivered at his touch. When the braid was undone, I realized I did feel cooler without the bonnet and without my hair being done up. A slight breeze stirred through the trees, and the combined shade made the temperature quite pleasant indeed.

But George wasn't finished. He threaded his fingers through my hair, standing close enough that our bodies were almost touching.

My heart was pounding wildly. I knew he was going to

try to kiss me again, but I couldn't allow it, no matter how much pleasure it would bring.

I stepped away from him, and his hand fell to his side.

"We shouldn't dally," I said, my breath nearly gone. "My parents will be wondering about the delay."

He just gazed at me, and I was not about to analyze the expression on his face, so I picked up my bonnet from the ground. "You can walk me home or stay here; it's your choice."

"Susannah," he said, his serious tone giving me pause. "Why have you been avoiding me?"

Any trite answer died on my lips. Maybe it was time to be straight with him, once and for all. It was probably better considering we might be neighbors for a while and would likely grow old together in the same town.

"I won't be one of your flirts, George," I said, meeting his gaze full-on. "I'm not like Anabel or Constance. I'm not looking for a convenient husband or some kissing in a barn. I was perfectly happy on my own before you came around, and I intend to stay that way. So the fact that you traded fixing my father's wagon to walk home with me tells me that you like a challenge and don't like to be told no. But I'm not going to be *your* challenge—someone for you to drop whenever you find a new pursuit." My hands were on my hips, and my chest heaving. To my dismay, I felt the tears start. I turned away, determined to put a good distance between us before any tears fell.

I took three steps before he caught my arm.

"Susannah, you're not one of my flirts." His other hand went around my waist, forcing me to turn toward him. "Those other women are just friendly, and if it makes you envious, then all the better.'"

I stared at him. "You're *trying* to make me jealous?" I

gave a hollow laugh. "How can I be jealous if I don't care what you do?"

He leaned down, his forehead nearly touching mine. "I think you do care."

I pulled my arm from his grasp and used both hands to push against his chest. "Even if I did care, I won't stand for it. I won't be a part of your games."

His hands grabbed mine, encircling them, and pulling me against him. "Then let's stop the games and get married."

I felt as if I'd stepped into a cold rainstorm.

I opened my mouth, but nothing came out. I tried to step away, to put some space between his words to me, but he wouldn't let go. He lowered his head and kissed my neck, then my jaw, then the heat of his mouth was on mine.

Since the first time he kissed me, I had tried to forget, but it all came rushing back in an instant. And if I thought his previous kiss was exhilarating, this kiss about made me pass out. It was familiar, yet new, and with all the stubbornness that had passed between us, there was a tenderness to George's passion.

I kissed him back. I couldn't help it. He'd just asked me to marry him, which told me that I wasn't his flirt and perhaps he wouldn't be spending the next thirty years walking a different woman home each Sabbath.

"Susannah, marry me," he whispered against my mouth, and I was lost again. His hands moved along my back, holding me closer than I thought was possible. It was almost as if clothing didn't separate us. "I'm not asking you lightly. I've been married before. I know what it takes, and I know what I want. I promise to never flirt with another woman again," he said, drawing back, then kissing my forehead, my cheeks, my eyelids. "Unless it will get you to kiss me back."

My eyes fluttered open. "You must not value your life."

He grinned. Finally, that grin was back. "My life is yours to do with what you will."

"You're a brave man."

"Perhaps," he said, his finger running along my face, then down my neck, and along my collarbone. A new heat started inside of me. "But I heard that love does strange things to a man."

I could barely breathe for the desire coursing through me. "Are you in love with me then, George?" Could it be true? What about his first wife? Was it like this between them?

"If it's not love, then I'm truly doomed for life to follow after every step you take."

"Even if those steps are short?" I said.

He chuckled. "I'll go at your pace . . . always." His hand moved up to my face, and thank goodness they did. I was about willing to let him break the commandments, if we hadn't already. "I'm crazy about you, Susannah, and I can't stop thinking about you—night or day. And if that's love, then I'm definitely in love with you."

"It might be love," I hedged. "But how will you know for sure?" I thought about his first wife again. Had he said these things to her, too?

His lips moved into a slow smile. "We could probably come up with some sort of a test."

I found I was caring less and less about what his relationship was like with his wife. I had him now, here, his arms around me. "Like pulling petals from a flower? Or writing me poetry?"

George's brows drew together. "Flowers are better." He stepped back and searched the ground for a wild flower. When he found a daisy, he picked it and held it out. One by one, he tugged off the petals: *she loves me . . . she does not . . . she loves me . . .*

I laughed when the last petal came up as *does not.*

"I guess that test failed," I said.

"No," he said, his eyes on me as he closed the distance between us. He broke off the end of the stem instead. "She does not."

With one petal left, the answer was clear. I stepped into his arms and let the world shrink to just the two of us. I whispered, "She loves you."

George lifted me up against him and kissed me achingly slow. When he broke away, every part of my body was numb. "It looks like I'll be needing to speak to your father."

[Following the tormenting of Susannah's specter upon the afflicted girls in the courthouse, who are showing extreme suffering]

Magistrate: Who do you think is their master?

Susannah: If they be dealing in the black art, you may know as well as I. I desire to lead myself according to the Word of God.

Magistrate: Is this according to God's Word?

Susannah: If I were such a person, I would tell you the truth.

Magistrate: How do you know? He that appeared in the shape of Samuel, a glorified saint, may appear in anyone's shape.

Magistrate: Do you believe these do not say true?

Susannah: They may lie, for aught I know.

Magistrate: May not you lie?

Susannah: I dare not tell a lie if it would save my life.

Magistrate: Then you will speak the truth?

Susannah: I have spoken nothing else. I would do them any good.

Magistrate: I do not think you have such affections for them whom just now you insinuated had the Devil for their master.

[Elizabeth Hubbard flinched and murmured that Susannah had pinched her hand. Others shouted that her specter was on a beam in the courthouse.]

Magistrate: Pray God discover you, if you be guilty.

Susannah: Amen. Amen. A false tongue will never make a guilty person.

—Susannah Martin's Examination, May 2, 1692
Adapted by Marilynne K. Roach, *The Salem Witch Trials*

CHAPTER 21

Salem Jail

THE NEXT FEW DAYS bring sweltering heat. It has not even been a week since Bridget Bishop was hanged, and we awake to the clanging of the metal door from the next cell. I sit up with a start, regretting the sharp movement. My neck throbs, and for a moment, I am disoriented.

Then I hear the clang again, and voices reach me.

"He is dead," says a man whose voice I don't recognize.

"What happened to him?" another voice. This one's the jailer's.

The other women in the cell are stirring, and I climb to my feet, aiding myself with the wall. As I shuffle to the bars to see what is going on in the neighboring cell, a new smell arises above the dank—the smell of death.

My heart sinks as I see the jailer drag Roger Toothaker from his cell. His once sturdy body is thin and brittle from only a month in jail. It doesn't take long for the body to fold in on itself in protectiveness. Mr. Toothaker's eyes are closed—a merciful observation. Does this mean he died in his sleep?

"Oh, Lord. Have mercy," Rebecca whispers, coming to stand by my side.

Mr. Toothaker's cell door is closed and locked, although his body remains in the corridor. A group of men have gathered, and I realize they are the coroner's jury. Holding their lanterns high and peering down at the body, one of them says, "His death is natural. He is an old man, after all."

The other men nod and continue staring down at the body for a moment.

Natural? I choke on the word. When has being imprisoned for witchcraft, starved, and neglected ever been a *natural* way to die?

"Contact his family," the coroner says. "If the family wants him back for burial, they can pay his jail bill first and carry him out themselves."

I watch in disbelief as the coroner and his men exit the jail and leave Roger Toothaker's body behind. Even in death, the man isn't given any respect.

I turn away from the scene of death and meet the gazes of Elizabeth and Rebecca. They've come to see for themselves what is going on.

"Is there nothing we can do?" Rebecca whispers.

The jailer is at the other end of the prison somewhere, so I say, "Let's wait to see if his family comes. If they don't, perhaps we can raise the money for a burial." Even as I speak, I know it is likely impossible. But how long will they leave Mr. Toothaker's body in the corridor?

A movement against my skirts startles me, and I look down to see little Dorothy clinging to the cell bars. She is staring at the body on the other side. What must be going through her head, I do not know, but it's impossible to protect her mind and eyes from the grim sights and sounds of our quarters.

"Come," I say to her in a gentle tone. She lets me take her hand and lead her deeper into the cell, away from Mr. Toothaker's lifeless body. Sarah Good has her eyes closed, her head resting in the crook of her thin arm.

I sit a few feet from Sarah Good and settle Dorothy on my lap. The little girl nestles against my breast, and for a moment, I feel comforted. If I could but close my eyes and imagine that I'm at home in Amesbury with a healthy grandchild curled on my lap. If I could but turn the fetid scents of human waste and rotted food to the smell of a fresh-plowed farm, new peas, and sunburned cheeks.

As it is, there is a small girl on my lap who needs as much comfort as I do. The women in our cell are either asleep or quiet. It seems we have become numb to the tragic death of Roger Toothaker, even before his body has been disposed of.

The sun rises, and the light shifts. If a morning meal is coming, it could still be hours away, and all we can do is wait. We cannot command anything or anyone. Waiting is our new life. Waiting to be fed. Waiting to be tried. Waiting for what comes next. From my vantage point, I can see the feet of Roger Toothaker, and I think on what I know of his life. Too little, I realize. Not enough. I should have spoken to him more. Perhaps offered him comfort. Perhaps found out about his family.

Now it is too late.

Rebecca Nurse comes and settles by me, her praying done for the time being. I glance over at her bent fingers, gnarled with age, spotted with wisdom. There is not much difference in our hands, as we were born in the same year.

She turns her head toward me and says softly, "This place takes the troublemaker out of all of us."

I am surprised at her statement, and it makes me smile. "Can't cause much trouble on this side of the bars."

Her return smile is faint, but it's there. "Tell me of who Susannah Martin is out in the world, who she is outside these walls."

"Calling me a troublemaker is highly accurate. I've never been one to keep my opinions to myself," I say. "My stepmother and my husband could certainly attest to that, if either of them were here today."

"When did it start for you?" Rebecca asks.

I look past her, to where Sarah Wildes is curled on her side, having fallen back asleep after the commotion Mr. Toothaker's death caused. "I suppose it's been over thirty years now. In 1660, we were living in Amesbury, and William Browne accused me of tormenting his wife, Elizabeth." I pause, the ridiculousness of it burning in my chest even now. "With my spirit, of course. As if my spirit had nothing better to do than float around and torment. Browne said I was the cause of his wife's insanity."

"Ah," Rebecca says. "What happened with the charges?"

"Nothing at the time," I say. "It just caused an upheaval with some of our neighbors, but I wasn't too fond of them anyway. Years later, my husband had to fight for my place in the Meeting House. Seems that some of my neighbors sided with Browne." I lift a shoulder, then sigh. "I shouldn't have dismissed it so easily though. Browne was one of my accusers."

Rebecca raises her eyebrows at this. "After all these years? What did he say?"

"The same things he said over thirty years ago," I say, leaning my head against the stone wall. "It's a wonder he remembered so much, but apparently, he spent the years thinking of little else. He claimed that I would appear at his house as a bird and peck at his wife's legs and torment her."

"And the court believed him."

I exhale slowly. "Yes. Although William Browne was not my only nemesis."

Across the cell, Sarah Wildes shifts in her sleep, then turns her head. Blinking her eyes open, she takes in the surrounding scene. Rebecca and I are the only ones awake in our cell, and Mr. Toothaker's body remains in the corridor, unclaimed.

Without a word, Sarah rises and comes over to sit by us, next to Rebecca.

I continue my story. "After the mess with William Browne, William Sargent Jr. became *my* tormenter." I shake my head at the memory. Even now, it seems unbelievable that a person could say such awful things about another person. "He claimed that I gave birth to an illegitimate baby and then killed it."

Rebecca stares at me, her eyes wide.

"I was arrested and put into jail. My husband, George, wouldn't stand for it, not for even one moment. The same day as my arrest, George filed suit against William Sargent for slander. And then George filed suit against William's brother, Thomas Sargent, who said equally nasty things."

"Like what?" Rebecca asks quietly, leaning closer to hear.

But I don't care who hears my story. All of the women in this cell have proved their merit. They will not accuse another in order to free themselves. "Thomas Sargent called my oldest son, Richard, an imp and my second son, George, a bastard."

"You were imprisoned because someone told lies about you?" Rebecca says with a shake of her head. "It seems our society has learned nothing."

"George posted the one-hundred-pound bond, and eventually the charges were dropped," I say, the events of that year still making my heart ache. "But the damage was done—far more than what was done by William Browne. Although William Sargent was found guilty of slander, my reputation never recovered."

"And you had Christopher Bartlett to deal with later," Rebecca says. She places her hand on my arm. "I'm very sorry."

I suppose I should see the irony in Rebecca Nurse offering comfort to her fellow-accused witch when she is also awaiting trial for witchcraft. I put my hand over hers and squeeze. "You are kind to apologize for the unapologetic."

Rebecca's smile is brief. There is too much pain surrounding us for a true smile.

"Tell me your story," I say.

"It's just as everyone else's. Life is full of challenges, and we but have to endure them." She pauses. "My sisters Mary Esty and Sarah Cloyce were imprisoned too. Many years ago, my mother was accused of witchcraft, although she was never convicted. I suppose the villagers believed she was guilty of witchcraft and passed it down to her daughters."

I blow out a breath. "Is that why you pray all of the time?"

Rebecca is quiet for a moment. "It might have been why I started, surely, but it brings me comfort in a world with very little comfort. With eight children, life is precarious."

"That I can agree with," I say.

"Francis and I married in 1644, and he built up a nice business of building wooden household items. We started out renting a farm of three hundred acres, but we were able to gradually buy it. He even served as an unofficial judge in Salem and as its constable."

"You sound like the perfect target for the Putnams with all that land."

"It's true. We were involved with a number of land disputes with the Putnam family." She clasps her hands together and says, "It was Edward and John Putnam who accused me first." Her voice trails off, and I think she is finished with her story, when she says, "I am innocent, Susannah, innocent like a child not yet born to this world."

I reach for her clasped hands and take them in my own. "I know. I believe you, Rebecca."

CHAPTER 22

Salisbury

THE WEDDING BANNS WERE read three Sabbath Meetings in a row. Of course my parents would never reject an offer made to their twenty-five-year-old daughter. They probably thought the day would never come. *I* thought the day would never come.

George started on our house right away. I told him we could live with my parents for a while or stay with his sister, but he was determined to build something for me. We had a house-raising, setting the simple frame in place, and then he spent every spare moment, sometimes far into the night, sawing and hammering.

After supper was cleared up, I'd often cross the field to watch him, handing him nails or doing odd jobs. The house was situated on the other side of the barn from the main house, and it was only two rooms. George said we'd get a bigger house later or he'd build more rooms on when the children came. Every time he said it, I blushed.

Little Hannah would stay with Goody Martin for now.

George said his sister needed something to do, something to keep her thriving.

As I approached the new house one evening in early July, I carried a rug that I'd tied. It would be the first article in our home. The kitchen area was complete, and as I came within view, I could hear the sound of the hammer coming from the single bedroom. I'd thought the wood planks were already set, so I wondered what George was doing.

I walked into the kitchen, marveling that this place would really be ours. It was covered in dust and bent nails at the moment, but by the time we married the next month, I'd have it tidy.

I entered the bedroom to find George building a bed frame. He was also shirtless, which I really couldn't blame him for. It was the hottest time of the year, and the heat didn't fade until long after the sun set.

George looked up and stopped hammering. My breath caught, and I knew it wasn't a good thing to be in our bedroom-to-be with him dressed like that—or rather, un-dressed. I hadn't seen him without a shirt since that day in the barn.

"You're here," he said, climbing to his feet. Perspiration glistened on his chest and arms, and I took a step back; he was a bit too male at the moment.

I unrolled the rug I'd brought and shook it out. "Do you like what I made?"

He walked toward me, making my heart pound, and I took another couple of steps back so that we were in the kitchen.

"I love it," he said, taking it from me and spreading it on the floor. "Looks perfect."

I admired the way the warm colors brightened the stark room already. I noticed a table that hadn't been there before. "You built a table, too?" I asked.

"I refurbished it, then I stained it," he said, leaning against the wall. I dragged my eyes away from his bare torso and examined the table. Things were coming together in this small house, and in just a few weeks I'd be Mrs. George Martin. It was strange to think about.

He came up behind me and wrapped his arms about my waist.

"You're sweaty," I said, not daring to lean back for more reasons than one.

"That's because I'm building us a bed," he said, right before he kissed my neck.

I wanted to turn in his arms and press my mouth against his, which was probably not the wisest thing since he was still half dressed. Instead, I pulled out of his grasp and walked to the door before he could stop me. Once outside, I skirted the house, George watching me from the doorway.

"It's looking like a real house now," I called to him.

He grinned at me as I inspected the exterior. "You're avoiding me, Susannah North."

I turned to face him, my hands on my hips. "Maybe you should put your shirt on, then."

He disappeared inside, then came back out a minute later, pulling on his shirt. "Better?"

No, but I said, "Yes."

He laughed and grabbed my hand, tugging it toward him, then kissed my palm. "Sorry to make you nervous."

"I'm fine," I said.

"Excellent," he said, leaning down and kissing my cheek. "I promise to be good, at least for a few more weeks."

My cheeks heated, and he laughed again. "Come on," he said. "I'll walk you home."

"Don't you need to finish what you were building?"

"You mean our *bed*? There's still an hour of light left. Do you want to stay?"

I couldn't get the image of his bare stomach out of my mind. "I don't think I should. Mother will be expecting me."

He slipped his hand into mine and nodded.

I felt fortunate to find a man who made me want to be with him every moment, yet didn't shy away from teasing me. But kissing him lately had been too intense, and even though we'd be married in a few weeks, I couldn't let my guard down now. And he seemed to have no such reservations. I wasn't sure what to make of that. He was certainly an experienced kisser; was he experienced at other things as well?

It had been on my mind more than I cared to admit. To think of him with his wife made me self-conscious.

George must have noticed I was quiet in thought. "It's just me, you know," he said, slowing his step. "George Martin—the man you're engaged to?"

I nodded but didn't say anything.

"You're not changing your mind, are you?" he said.

I looked up at him, and I was surprised at the genuine worry in his eyes. "Why would you say that?" But even as I spoke, I knew I didn't sound too convincing.

"Because you won't let me kiss you," he said softly.

How could I tell him my worries? Would he laugh? Think I was a silly woman? Tell me it was none of my business?

"We do kiss," I said.

"For the last couple of weeks, you've turned away," he said. "I didn't want to make it a big concern, but I'd like to know why." His fingers released mine, and he stopped walking.

I took a couple of more steps, thinking of what I could say without sounding like a silly, naive woman. He walked to me and brushed my cheek with his fingertips. "Talk to me, Susannah. You've never had trouble before."

I stared at the ground, willing my eyes not to burn with tears. He'd always been a flirt; I'd known that since day one. But from the moment we were engaged, I hadn't seen him talking to the other women like he used to, at least nothing more than simple friendliness. Maybe I was overreacting. Maybe this was what they called cold feet.

But seeing the house almost complete and George working on our bed frame, half dressed, I realized that he would, indeed, be my husband. And I would be his wife. Was I ready to be so intimate with him? To change my identity for a man?

"Susannah," he whispered, his fingers tipping up my chin.

The tears had fallen, and he brushed them away.

My throat hitched, and finally the words came. "You're too good of a kisser for it to be innocent. You've been married before. You're experienced where I am not. For all I know, you could have been with a whole string of women before marrying."

He looked surprised, but that wasn't any indication of innocence. "Are you asking which other women I've kissed?"

I nodded, then shook my head. I was too embarrassed to continue this conversation. I turned from him, but his hand was on my arm.

"I kissed a few women before marrying Hannah. But none of them were like you, and none of them made me feel like you make me feel." He paused. "Not even Hannah, although she was a great woman and a great mother."

I let that settle into my heart. It made me feel a little better, but I was still unsure.

"What about our wedding night?" I couldn't look at him. My cheeks were so hot. "Will you be laughing at me?"

His arms came around me, and he kissed my forehead. "Never."

I looked up at him then, to see the truth in his eyes for myself. "Promise?"

"Of course. You don't have anything to worry about with me. What about you? What other men have you been with?"

I pushed against his chest. "How dare you ask me that, George Martin!"

He lifted his hands in surrender. "You asked *me*. How is that different?"

I was smoldering, both with relief and something else I didn't recognize. "You know you are the first man I've kissed." My stubbornness had kicked in, but it was better than my painful doubts.

George grabbed me, laughing. I squirmed against him, but finally settled in his arms. "You'll be safe with me," he whispered in my ear.

My face flushed, the heat spreading through my whole body. I released a sigh and let him hold me.

"Don't be nervous," he said.

"I'm not nervous," I said. But I was.

"I'll take care of you." He kissed me on the cheek, soft and sweet. "Trust me."

I wanted to cling to him, but I knew better than to start something that would lead to other things.

"I love you, Susannah. Don't forget that," he said, as if he still felt compelled to convince me.

"I love you, too." I let my hand slip into his. We didn't talk the rest of the way to my house, but we didn't need to. Our hearts were in unison.

CHAPTER 23

Salisbury

THE MORNING OF MY wedding on August 11, I woke with a pounding headache. It might have had something to do with the fact that I was up half the night, sewing and restitching the dress I'd made over from my sister Mary's dress. The alteration was not working. We were simply too different, and I regretted even trying to make it work.

Finally, I gave up in the early morning hours and fell into a fitful sleep.

The sun was streaming through my east window when I opened my eyes next, and I sat up with a start. My dress was nowhere near finished, and after seeing the crumpled heap on the straight-backed chair, I knew it was hopeless. I'd have to wear my Sabbath dress.

"Susannah," my mother called from the hallway as she approached my room. Her eyes widened when she stepped into my room. "You're not even up yet." She looked from me to the dress. "What's going on?"

Tears burned in my eyes, and I took a stuttering breath.

"I tried to alter it, but it just won't fit. I'll be wearing my Sabbath dress."

Mother's face pulled into a frown. "If I would have known sooner, we could have purchased fabric in town."

"No," I said. "We can't afford it, and there wasn't time to make something new, anyway."

I climbed off my bed and took down my Sabbath dress from its peg.

"I wish I would have brought my dress over from England," she said.

My parents had sold everything they could to buy passage.

Mother opened her hand and revealed a cameo brooch her mother had given her. "You can wear this today—it will look lovely on whichever dress you choose."

She had worn it on her wedding day, and I knew it was her most valuable possession. "Thank you," I said, hugging her. Mother was not a very affectionate person, but I couldn't let this moment pass without an embrace. George had taught me that more than anything.

Feeling downhearted, I heated water over the oven fire and filled up the bathing tub in the kitchen. I would be married this afternoon, yet I'd be dressed like any other Sabbath day. Mother crushed dried lavender in the water, then she left the room so I could have privacy. My father would remain in the fields until early afternoon when it was time for him to get washed up to go into town.

I undressed, then settled into the warm water. Tomorrow morning at this time, I'd be a married woman—a woman experienced in love.

I flushed at the thought. I bent my head forward, letting my hair float on the surface of the water, then I let my fingers pull the strands beneath the surface. The scented water felt heavenly, and I slid lower in the tub, letting the water rush over me.

Then I scrubbed my scalp and rinsed out the lather. Mary would be coming by to fix my hair, so at least I'd have one thing special for this day. By the time I climbed out of the tub and dried myself with a cloth, I felt more relaxed and less frustrated about not having a real wedding dress.

By the time I had dressed, I heard Mary's wagon pulling up. I flung open the front door and hurried to her side to help her down from the wagon. She was positively glowing in her pregnancy state.

"Oh," she said, her eyes narrowing as she studied me. "You're wearing that."

"Don't give me grief, now. I've barely slept at all trying to get your dress to work. There's nothing for it, though."

Mary pursed her lips and bustled inside the house, as much as her awkward shape would let her. She headed straight for my bedroom and picked up her discarded gown. I came in beside her, my arms folded across my chest.

She examined the dress for a moment, then turned to face me. "You're right. There's nothing more to be done. I was sure it could be remade." She sank to the bed and held it against her chest. "It was a lovely dress."

"Sorry I picked half of it apart," I said, sitting next to her on the bed. "Perhaps I can stitch it back together, and you can pass it on to your daughters someday."

Mary gave a small shrug, and she glanced at the door, then back to me. "Did Mother give you a talking-to about the wedding night?" she asked.

The back of my neck felt warm. "I'm twenty-five, Mary, not a girl of seventeen or eighteen. I know a thing or two."

"Oh?" She raised her brows so high they nearly touched her hairline. "Do you? Have you been up to no good?"

I slapped her arm. "Of course not. I meant that I don't need any advice from you, and especially not *Mother*."

Her mouth stretched into a smile. "George will school you, eh?"

"Mary!" I stood and crossed the room, putting distance between us. "It's none of your concern."

Mary raised her hands and laughed. "All right. I'll be quiet. But if you have any questions, I'll be happy to tell you how to please your husband."

My mouth dropped open then, and she stood and left my room, carrying her wedding dress with her. I stared after her. Should I ask my sister for some words of wisdom? *No*, I thought. I couldn't stand her knowing what my questions might be.

By the time we reached the Meeting House, my heart would not stop pounding. My hair had been intricately braided by Mary and intertwined with flowers, and I wore my mother's cameo with my pale blue Sabbath dress.

I noticed right away that the Martins' wagon had not arrived, and my breathing doubled. What if he changed his mind? What if something befell them on the ride there? Wedding guests had already arrived, most of them friends of my parents.

Orlando came to greet me, leaning in to kiss my cheek. It was very forward of him, and I blushed, but his smile was sweet. I saw Constance in the background, a smile on her face. It seemed the two were getting on well together, and I was pleased for them both.

The magistrate arrived, and still the Martins were not there. Now I knew that my mother was worried, although my father looked quite unfazed. Mary sidled up to me and grasped my hand. She didn't need to speak; we were both thinking the same thing.

I left the Meeting House and stood in the hot afternoon sun that was sliding west. And then I saw the wagon. Relief pulsed through me, loosening the knots in my stomach.

All the Martins were in the wagon. Little Hannah sat between George and Goody Martin. My heart soared. There had been talk of Eve coming, but neither my mother nor I took it seriously. We had not seen Goody Martin at more than two Sabbath Meetings since they moved here.

My gaze met George's, and my heart soared anew. It was as if the love I knew he felt for me reached across the space between us as if no one else was around. I wanted to be with him, and him only, while everyone else faded away.

The noise of surrounding greetings came back into focus, and I was once again in the present time. I walked forward to take Goody Martin's arm, and she handed me an arrangement of flowers. "For your bridal bouquet."

They were beautiful and fresh. "Thank you," I said.

George took her other arm, and we smiled at each other. My heart felt as if it had been stitched to his as we caught each other's gazes over his sister's bonnet. My mother joined us and reached for little Hannah. The young girl was immediately content in her future grandmother's arms, surprising me because she hadn't warmed to me yet.

Once inside the Meeting House, Goody Martin sank onto a bench toward the front, her breathing labored, but a smile on her face.

I was swept away by my family, with no chance to speak to George. The magistrate stood at the front of the room, his expression quite serious, matching his austere black robes. A hush fell over the gathering as George walked up to the front of the room to stand by the magistrate.

When he was in place, I linked my arm with my father's, and we walked up the aisle as well. I glanced at my mother, then had to look away from her tear-stained face. I felt my eyes burn and knew I'd be crying if I looked at my mother again.

I kept my eyes on George, but that wasn't much better.

His gray eyes were dark today, perhaps because we were inside, or because he was wearing his best suit. My pale blue dress complimented his dark jacket, perhaps in a way that Mary's made-over wedding dress wouldn't have. His gaze drew me in, and I was suddenly impatient.

My father released me, and I took my place on the other side of the magistrate.

"George Martin," the magistrate said. "Doest thou take Susannah North to be thy wife?"

My breath hitched as I waited for George's response. His voice was clear when he said, "Yes, I do."

The magistrate turned to me and said, "Susannah North, doest thou accept George Martin as thy husband?"

I met George's gaze, and my heart expanded. One word from me and we'd be husband and wife in the eyes of God. There was no doubt what that word would be. "Yes," I said.

"By the law of Massachusetts," the magistrate pronounced, "thou art now husband and wife."

George held his hand toward me, his eyes boring into mine. I placed my hand in his, immediately enveloped by his strong warmth. George drew me toward him, and I blushed, knowing what he was about to do.

He kissed me in front of everyone, and it wasn't just a peck. When he drew away, my face was on fire, not to mention the rest of my body. We were then surrounded by parents and siblings, and the congratulations were underway.

Mercy Lewis: You have been a long time coming to the court today. You can come fast enough in the night.

Susannah: No sweetheart.

John Indian: It was that woman. She bites. She bites.

Magistrate: Have you not compassion for these afflicted?

Susannah: No. I have none.

[The court tempted a touch test. Abigail Williams, Mary Walcott, and Goody Bibber were all repelled.]

Magistrate: What is the reason these cannot come near you?

Susannah: I cannot tell. It may be the Devil bears me more malice than another.

Magistrate: Do you not see how God evidently discovers you?

Susannah: No. Not a bit for that.

Magistrate: All the congregation think so.

Susannah: Let them think what they will.

—Susannah Martin's Examination, May 2, 1692
Adapted by Marilynne K. Roach, author of *The Salem Witch Trials*

CHAPTER 24

Salem Jail

WHEN ROGER TOOTHAKER'S body is collected by his family, the women in the cell seem to breathe easier. But that only lasts a day or two, and then the sense of foreboding returns, even fiercer than before. For the end of June is approaching, and with it, the dates of our trials. Sarah Good's is set for June 28, and June 29 mine and Rebecca Nurse's. June 30 is the date for Sarah Wildes and Elizabeth Howe. In just a matter of three days, we will all know our fate.

Guilty or not guilty?

The days pass slowly. The heat swelters and lice has spread to each of us, no longer just contained to little Dorothy. The girl has spent more and more time on my lap, and I am happy to wrap my arms around her and pull her close.

When Sarah Good is awake, she paces the cell. When she is asleep, we all breathe a sigh of relief. At least she is eating and moving again, although I wonder if it only means that her grief has deepened another layer.

The night before Sarah Good's trial, I'm not the only one who can't sleep. Elizabeth Howe stands near the bars, looking out into the dark corridor. I rise and cross to her. "What is it?" I ask.

She doesn't answer, merely lifts a shoulder. Several moments pass, and I'm about to go and lay back down when she says, "If you could live your life differently, what would you have done? Would you have married someone else? Would you have had fewer children? Moved to another town?"

I think of my father and mother, my stepmother, my sister Mary and my sister Sarah. All are gone now. I think of George and the first day I saw him when he was plowing our field. How his gray-blue eyes seemed to look at me and say, "I choose you." How when my stubborn heart finally softened and I chose him back, nothing ever seemed more important but the life we lived together—the sorrows, the aches, the joys, the grandchildren. We stood together, hand in hand, and faced the trials of life. For better or for worse.

George is gone now, yet I still feel his presence. He has not left me, nor will he ever.

"No," I whisper. "I would not have married anyone but George."

Elizabeth nods and reaches out for the bars, wrapping her fingers around their cold solidness. "Even with my husband's blindness, I would not have changed my decisions." She pauses. "But being in here has given me a chance to reflect on some of my own reactions to others. How we treat each other. How we judge each other."

"How we lie about each other," I finish.

"And for what?" Elizabeth says.

I don't think she expects an answer—who knows the answer, anyway?—but I say, "We are afraid. Afraid of life and of death. Afraid of another being stronger or wealthier or happier than we are. So we tear them down."

Elizabeth lets out a sigh. "You are right. And tomorrow, it will begin with Sarah Good."

We are quiet for another moment. The night sounds of the jail cell creak around us. The skitter of a rat, the soft snore of one of our cellmates, and the ever pressing darkness that makes the quietest sounds new and sharp.

Elizabeth goes to lie down, yet I remain at the bars. When the footsteps come, I am relieved, yet fearful at the same time. How much longer can this all last? How much longer will George visit me?

When his face comes into view in the murky darkness, my heart aches anew. The lines around his eyes and mouth are ones that I am so familiar with. They represent our years together, working side by side, raising our children, loving each other, fighting with each other. Forgiving each other.

"Susannah," his voice whispers around me, reaching into my soul. "I've been waiting for you to come home."

I reach for his hands and close my eyes. If only he could take me into his arms. "This cannot last forever," I say at last.

He squeezes my fingers, and I feel the tears start to burn in my eyes.

"The children were here. They brought food, and they all looked well."

He only nods. Of course he can visit them anytime he wants. "And you?"

"I am managing," I say. I tell him of Sarah Good's infant. Of Roger Toothaker. Of the trials beginning tomorrow. "If something happens to me, you will not leave me, will you?"

His mouth moves into a smile that I know so well. "I would never leave you. I will wait as long as I need to, until you are released and can come home."

I know he is not speaking of our farm. And I know there is nothing I'd like more than to join him in his heavenly sphere. Even if I were to be exonerated and allowed to return to my farm and rejoin my children, I fear I am too broken to survive the journey.

As the morning approaches, George is gone, and Sarah Good wakes well before the jailer comes to fetch her. I expect her to be quiet and moody, to pace the cell, to grumble and curse, to shun her daughter. But instead, she sits close to me and starts to talk.

"The court will pick apart my life," she begins in a breathless voice as she twists her hands.

I almost fear this agitated Sarah Good over the despondent one. "We will be here, praying for you."

Sarah does not seem to let that sink in. "My father committed suicide, you know. My stepfather stole my inheritance, and I let my displeasure be known at that."

I, more than anyone, understand. I'd spent years fighting the courts for control over my father's property, only to lose in the end.

"My first husband died, and our debts were insurmountable," she says. "And then my current husband couldn't support a family either, and now he accuses me. Samuel and Mary Abbey took us in when we were homeless, and nothing went right. They blamed me for their sick cattle and sheep and hogs."

Her voice rises, waking the others in the cell. I don't shush her, because it will all come out at court today, and what does it matter if the surrounding prisoners hear?

"I was blamed for Thomas Gage's cows that died, and when my cousin Zachariah Herrick wouldn't put us up, I might have cursed his cattle." She is speaking faster now, and I barely catch all that she is saying. "But I was angry. I have no power over animals."

Her eyes are wide—wild—dark—and she twists her hands furiously. "Those girls say that I float around and afflict them. Do you see me float around? Have you seen my spectral?"

I shake my head, but still she is not satisfied and continues to rant.

By the time the jailer collects Sarah Good, she has run out of words. She pushes past her daughter and walks out of the cell, her head hanging, her eyes empty.

An hour later when she returns, there is no need for any of to ask what the verdict of her trial was.

The deadness of her expression tells us all.

Sarah has been found guilty of witchcraft and sentenced to death.

God help us all.

CHAPTER 25

Salisbury

AFTER THE WEDDING MEAL, my parents ushered George and me to their wagon. They'd be riding back with Goody Martin and little Hannah. Just before handing me up, George drew me against him and whispered, "Let's walk."

My heart thumped as I remembered the first time he walked me home from the Meeting House, and how he'd proposed. "All right," I said.

George informed my parents that we were walking, and we set out, congratulations trailing us. I carried my bridal flowers in one hand and George's hand with my other. We waved to the wagons as they passed us and smiled at the parting congratulations.

Then, finally, it was quiet, and George and I walked in silence as the sun sank beneath the horizon. The heat of the day finally released its hold, and I didn't feel like I was standing inside a cast-iron stove anymore. Except that George's hand in mine was starting the warmth up again as he absentmindedly stroked the back of my hand with his thumb.

Which was driving me crazy. We were married now, and I didn't have to tell him to hold back. The nerves had returned, knotting in my stomach. I tried to focus on the twilight spreading over the farms. The deep green of tall plants nearing harvest against the violet sky was beautiful. The temperature was perfect, and George must have noticed too because he said, "We should sleep under the stars tonight."

At first I thought he was fooling me, but when I looked up, his expression was serious and intense. It made my breath catch because we *could* sleep under the stars together.

"What do you think, Mrs. Martin?" he said, brushing my chin with his fingers.

My step slowed at his touch. "I think that would be fine, Mr. Martin."

He smiled and lowered his head until his lips were only a couple of inches from mine. "Good, the moon should be plenty bright tonight."

He didn't kiss me, but I blushed anyway at his words. He merely straightened and continued walking, my hand in his.

By the time we passed my parents' home, it was nearly dark, and when we reached our two-room house, the moon had started to rise. George had been right; it was nearly a full moon, so its pale light glimmered over the fields.

"Wait here," George said, opening the front door and leaving me on the porch, at least what was to be a porch soon. It was halfway finished. Moments later, George returned with the rug I'd made and the quilt off the top of our new bed.

He was serious about sleeping outside. I laughed. He winked at me and stepped off the porch, then found a grassy spot near a tree to lay down the rug.

"What about a pillow?" I asked.

"That's what I'm for."

"All right, I need to change, then." I entered the house and made my way through the dark to the back bedroom. There was enough glow from the moon that I didn't light a candle. My mother had brought over a satchel of clothing that morning with my nightgown and other necessities.

I didn't hear a sound from George, which meant he hadn't followed me inside. I removed my nightgown and shook it out. I'd added some ribbon and lace to it this past week, hoping to make it prettier. But now, as I undressed, I wished I had something new to wear.

I pulled the nightgown over my head, the softness of the well-washed fabric settling over my curves. And then with a deep breath, and a small prayer, I walked out onto the porch.

George whistled from where he was sitting on the rug, the quilt pulled up to his waist. He'd taken off his jacket and shirt, his bare chest showing in the moonlight. My mouth went dry. What if he'd completely undressed and wore nothing beneath that quilt?

I almost turned back around to give myself more time to let my heart rate slow. Instead, I stepped off the porch and walked toward him.

He lifted the edge of the quilt, saying nothing, but I did see he still had his trousers on. I relaxed a bit and sat down on the rug. George pulled me toward him, and I nestled my head against his shoulder. I wasn't quite sure what I should do with my hands at first, but George took care of that for me.

He drew my arm across his bare stomach, until my hand rested against his opposite side, touching his warm, breathing skin. I closed my eyes as his hand trailed along my shoulder, then down the length of my arm.

His fingers moved back up to my shoulder, then slowly along my back and side. When they brushed the swell of my breast, I thought I might start on fire. Was he just planning to torture me until I begged him to take me?

But then I noticed that his breathing was about as scant as mine. I lifted up, using my hand to brace myself against his torso. His eyes were half open, watching me.

"Susannah," he whispered. "I love you."

I smiled, then pressed my mouth against his. The nervous knot in my stomach had changed to an ache—stronger than I could have imagined, and it was for George. I wanted him to never let me go.

His mouth captured mine as he turned to his side and drew our bodies together. It was then that I knew there had never been anyone but George for me, and there would never be anyone else.

CHAPTER 26

Salisbury

"YOU HAVE CAST A spell over me," George whispered in my ear.

I ran my fingers over the morning stubble on his face. Was it possible to tire of kissing a man? With George, I could not imagine a time that I would not crave his touch.

He lifted his head, his eyes soaking me in. We were in our new house, the day after our wedding, having given up sleeping outside when it was clear we wouldn't be sleeping anyway. Sometime toward dawn, we both dozed in our new bed, but now the sunlight streamed through our window, and I knew we'd missed at least two meals.

His gaze moved down the length of my body, and I found myself blushing.

"You are beautiful, Susannah."

"You are too," I whispered back, and he started to kiss me again, taking his time, moving from my mouth to my neck.

"We can't stay all day in bed," I said.

"No, we can't," George murmured, occupied with other things. "I was planning at least a week."

I laughed. "Our families will send for the constable."

"As long as they arrest us both and keep us in the same cell, I'll be happy," he said.

I ran my fingers through his hair. "I would miss our bed in the cell. I hear the prisoners sleep on the ground."

"That's only for the mild criminals. For the true criminals, they chain them to the walls."

I shuddered. Was George just teasing me? I didn't find out because he kissed me again, and all conversation became lost.

By the afternoon, even George couldn't remain in bed any longer. There was too much to do, plus there was the promise of another night in our wedding bed, and another night after that, followed by forever.

The cellar was the first thing George set out to finish. He had it halfway dug out when I had supper ready. We were only eating cooked potatoes and beans, but George acted like it was a feast for a king. He made me laugh with his enthusiasm.

"You are an excellent cook, Susannah," George said, after taking his first bite.

"I'm about as good as any woman, I suppose," I said and started eating. There was nothing special about my cooking, and George knew it, but it was nice to be complimented.

His sister and his daughter would be returning to the house on the morrow, and we both recognized the fact. For after dinner, George didn't go back outside to work on the cellar. Instead, he reached for my hand and said, "Cleaning up can wait. I want to spend the evening with only you."

His arms encircled my waist, and I forgot all plans to tidy the kitchen or scrub pots. I let him lead me to our bedroom and untie my apron.

Goose pimples broke out on my arms as he started to undo the fasteners to my blouse. "I'm going to be pregnant the first week of our marriage if you keep this up, George."

His lips were hot on my neck, and his words came out a mumble. "We will have a dozen children, then."

I turned in his arms and wrapped my hands around his neck. Every part of me was warm, and George's touch made me feel as if I were surrounded by the softest down feathers. Comforted. Loved. I smiled up at him. "Life is not all about pleasure."

His eyebrows lifted slightly, and his mouth curved into a smile. "Every day with you as my wife will be a pleasure, Susannah." His mouth brushed against mine. "There will be hard times, yes, as life is hard, but we will face them together."

I kissed him back, then I drew away once again. "Will you always take my side, George, even when you don't agree with me?"

His laugh was soft. He picked up my hands and linked our fingers together. "I promise. I will always be on your side."

And I believed him with my whole heart.

In the spring of the year about eighteen years since Susanna Martin came unto our house at Newbury from Amesbury in an Extraordinary dirty season when it was not fit for any person to travel, she then came on foot. When she came into our house I asked her whether she came from Amesbury a foot, she said she did. I asked her how she could come in this time a foot and bid my children make way for her to come to the fire to dry herself. She replied she was as dry as I was and turned her coats on side and I could not perceive that the sole of her shoes were wet. I was startled at it that she should come so dry and told her that I should have been wet up to my knees if I should have come so far on foot. She replied that she scorned to have a drabbled tail.

—Sarah Atkinson, age 48

CHAPTER 27

Salem Jail

THE DAY OF MY trial, June 29, dawns early. I will go to court with Rebecca Nurse and we will both stand trial for witchcraft. We are not allowed to have lawyers represent us, so we will represent ourselves. I stand in the middle of the cell and look around at the women who have been with me these past months. We have cried together, starved together, and told our stories to each other. What hope that might have been in Sarah Good's eyes for herself has long since fled, but I can see that she still hopes for me and Rebecca.

Sarah Good grasps my hand and says, "May the Lord be with you." Her words are the most sincere thing I've ever heard her say.

I nod, my throat growing thick with emotion. Now is not the time to let tears fall. I must stay strong and not let the court think that I've changed my mind about my confession. Elizabeth Howe crosses to me and hugs me. Dorothy wraps her thin arms around me, and I hug her back. Sarah Wildes embraces me as well.

The jailer binds my hands together and leads me out of the cell, with Rebecca following. I peer up at the blue sky as we are led to the Court of Oyer and Terminer where the Grand Jury awaits. Has the sky ever been so blue? The sun ever so golden? I try to memorize the green of the trees, the rich brown of the earth, but all too soon we step into the courtroom. The place goes silent, and a hundred pairs of eyes stare at us.

My breath cuts out when I realize all that have assembled—neighbors and former accusers. How did they all get here? How did they all know? And it's then I realize that these people want me dead. Gone and buried. And they will stand up in a court of law to speak lies so that it will be so.

As if I were looking at a picture book, images flash through my mind as I scan the crowd. I will not look away. I will not hang my head. If I am to be accused, I want the accusers to look me in the eye.

As I'm led to the front of the room to stand before the jury, I look over at the girls who have gathered. The moment I look at them, they cry out and twist their bodies as if they are possessed by some demon. My blood churns at the sight of such foolishness. It takes a few moments for the courtroom to quiet down. I am asked to enter my plea, and I say, "Not guilty."

I stand still, my dress hanging limply about me, and listen as the court reads the account of my May 2 examination and how I had laughed when they told me of the accusations. Yes, I had laughed at those accusations, and at the fact anyone could believe I was somehow tormenting strange girls I'd never met. As the charges are read now, almost two months later, the girls continue to act as if I am attacking them while, at the same time, I'm standing in the courtroom with my hands bound together.

Lieutenant John Allen is called forward, and he tells the jury of a time when he'd refused to let his ox carry a load for me. I remember this well, and the disbelief that had shot through me at the time.

"When she told me that my oxen wouldn't be of any use to me if I didn't help her, I became upset," John Allen says, his deep voice resonating through the court so that all are paying close attention to him. "I called her a witch—well deserved, I say. My oxen needed their rest and to feed in the meadow."

I stare at him as he speaks, willing him to meet my eyes, but he is focused on the jury as he continues, "When I came back to fetch my oxen, all sixteen had left and crossed the river. They swam to Plum Island, and I wasn't able to catch them for two days. Fourteen of them plunged into the ocean and only one survived." He turns to look at me now.

Raising his hand, he says, "We have been tormented by this witch long enough."

The girls gasp and convulse, and I remain still. Others come forward, and my head is spinning. Jarvis Ring stands before the jury and says, "Seven years ago, I was held motionless in the dark by something. It bit my finger, and I realized it was the specter of Susannah Martin." He holds up his hand. "The bite never healed, and you can still see the marks."

I want to laugh. But mostly I want to scream. How can a court of people believe any of this?

John Pressy is called forward, and he tells the court, "Years ago, it was about twenty-four, I reckon, I became lost in the area near the Martins' land on a Sabbath eve. I saw a moving light that was as big as a bushel basket. It accosted me and ruffled like a turkey cock when I prodded it with my stick."

The jury stares intently at John Pressy, as do I.

"I panicked and whacked at it, but I couldn't get it to leave me alone. I tried to get away, and I fell into a hole. When the light disappeared, I saw Susannah Martin watching me." He turns his head toward me but doesn't meet my gaze. "It was she who caused the blows."

One after another, people testify against me. William Browne, from my past, is now in the courtroom, eager to tell of how I made his wife go insane. "Susannah was acquitted of the charges against my wife, and Susannah continued to torment her. When I returned home from a journey, I found my wife distempered and frenzied in mind. Every doctor told us that she'd been bewitched."

The testimonies continue. Joseph Ring, Nathaniel Clark, and Joseph Knight all stand to testify. And finally, Sarah Atkins comes forward.

The woman had once been a friend. Now, I resent that I ever knew her and that she can stand in court, dressed in clean clothes, well fed and healthy, while I must live in a cell not fit for animals. Goody Atkins tells the court how I walked to her home and managed to keep my skirts and shoes dry although the roads were wet and muddy.

I know there is nothing I can say that will refute these people. They will believe what they do, and they will think they saw what they saw. They have not come here today to stand up for my character, but to break it down until it's nothing but dust under their feet. They do not have the courage to speak the truth, but rather they'd join in with the other accusers so that they, themselves, might be seen as innocent.

Fear drives men and women to do mad things.

I do not know how much time has passed, nor do I know the number of those who've testified against me. But when I am asked if I have anything to answer to those who have testified against me, I can only speak the truth: "I have led a most virtuous and holy life."

The sounds in the courtroom are dull around me as I am led to a chair. It's as if my mind cannot take in any more accusations. Someone could be screaming them at me, but I doubt I'd hear them. I'm unable to soak one more thing in for comprehension.

Rebecca Nurse will stand trial next, but for now, I have said all I can. I have been accused. I have pleaded not guilty. And now I await my sentencing.

It comes in moments.

I am found guilty. Sentenced to hanging.

If I thought the courtroom mad and chaotic during my trial, it becomes like hell's fury when Rebecca Nurse stands and faces her accusers. The voices come and go, and I catch bits and pieces of the accusations flung at Rebecca.

Goody Sarah Bibber clutches at her knees and cries that she is being pricked by Rebecca. Widow Sarah Holten testifies that her husband's blindness, choking spells, and stomach pain were caused by Rebecca after the Holtens' pigs wandered onto her property. Mr. Holten died as a result of the inflictions by Rebecca.

I can no longer listen, no longer comprehend. The minutes wear on, and the testimonies blend together. But then something changes. John Putnam Sr. and his wife counter the spectral reports.

Rebecca's two daughters, Rebecca Preston and Mary Tarbell, tell the court that their mother's physical infirmity is not a witchmark after all. Abigail and Deliverance Hobbs are brought forward, and Rebecca is stunned to see them. She turns and says, "What? Do you bring her? She is one of us."

The jurors erupt into whispers, and my heart sinks. I

know that Rebecca isn't condemning herself or admitting that both she and Deliverance are witches. She sees a woman who was also falsely accused, yet has turned on the rest of us and lies so that she might be free. When the commotion fades, others step forward and testify in behalf of Rebecca's character, and I watch as the jury is swayed.

At last. Someone will be saved. It won't be me or Sarah Good, but Rebecca Nurse will be spared execution.

Rebecca stands as the jury deliberates. Around us, the court buzzes with whispers and hot looks in our direction. Rebecca and I don't have to sit side by side or speak. We know each other's thoughts. She is sorry that I have been found guilty. I am praying that she is not.

Thomas Frisk, the foreman, walks before the jury, and everyone grows quiet. "Rebecca Nurse has been found *not* guilty."

If my hands were free, I'd throw them around her neck. Rebecca doesn't move, doesn't even blink, as an uproar overtakes the court. The girls shriek, convulsing in their chairs until they collapse onto the floor.

The jurors and the court members stare at the girls and their twisted limbs in horror.

My stomach twists as well.

They are whispering amongst themselves, and a wave of dread pushes through me. Some of the jurors are making no secret that they are questioning Rebecca's comment of "she is one of us." Then one of the jurors says, "In light of this new affliction upon the girls since we gave the verdict, we will have to reconsider our decision."

And then the court calls a recess and leaves the bench. We are forced to stay in our places and wait. What has happened? One of the judges looks over at us and says he is not satisfied with the verdict. Another judge comes quite close to us and says for all to hear that Rebecca will need to be held accountable for the latest inflictions on the girls who had been writhing only moments before.

I have been sentenced; only a miracle from God can save me now. So I pray for Rebecca. I pray that she will have her miracle. The moments that follow are perhaps the longest in my life. If I thought waiting in prison for my trial was long, I was mistaken.

Rebecca Nurse is forced to stand again and to await the return of the jury.

When the jurors return, all eyes are focused on them. I can barely breathe, knowing that in moments, we will know the fate of my friend.

The jurors seat themselves and face Rebecca. One of them asks about her comment to Deliverance Hobbs. I watch Rebecca and wonder what she'll answer. *Defend yourself,* I plea silently.

She remains quiet. Her shoulders are thin and hunched. Her face is pale, and her hands tremble.

"Goody Nurse," a juror says. "What do you have to say in defense of the accusations made against you?"

The court is quiet, waiting. Rebecca says nothing at all.

The moments pass, and finally, the words, "We've revised our verdict of 'not guilty.' The court finds Goody Nurse guilty of witchcraft."

CHAPTER 28

Salisbury

I BLAMED OUR FIRST married argument on the heat of the summer. George had spent the day sanding the flooring of our house, and I had taken the horse and cart into town to get a few supplies for us, in addition to what Mother requested. Hannah elected to stay with Mother; it seemed they'd formed a bond that I'd yet to share with the little girl. It was a new experience for me to shop in town as a married woman. I supposed I should have expected the questions that came my way, but I hadn't expected the looks of curiosity from practically everyone.

"Oh, you're out shopping, are you?" Mistress Beedle stopped me outside the general store. Her gaze went from my face to my toes. "I didn't think you'd be out and about so soon after marrying."

What did she mean by that? It was as if she could see right through me and knew that I was no longer a virgin and had been sleeping with my own husband. Yes, I realized that George had been considered a catch for more than one woman, and somehow I was the one who caught him. Me: stocky, short, buxom, and definitely not the prettiest woman in Salisbury.

I flushed, although I wasn't sure exactly why I should feel that way. "We're in need of a few supplies," I said. "George has nearly finished building our house."

Her brows lifted in curiosity. "It will be lovely to see it once it's all finished. One bedroom, eh?"

"For now," I said, feeling another blush heat my face. "Hannah is staying with Goody Martin at the main house. We didn't want her to have too many changes at once."

Mistress Beedle pursed her lips. "I suppose that's convenient for you—not having to worry about your new stepdaughter too much."

"Oh, she's with us a lot," I said, trying to keep the edge out of my voice. If I were impertinent, my mother would be sure to hear all about it. But Mistress Beedle didn't seem too impressed by anything I had to say, and it was all I could do not to be rude to her.

Inside the general store, I saw Constance. Now that she was sweet on Orlando Bagley, it would be easier to talk to her. Her gaze was piercing as she said, "You look like you've had a lot of sun."

"I'm helping George where I can on building our new house."

Constance leaned close. "How is it? Being married and all?"

"It's wonderful," I said truthfully, but I wouldn't give her any more than that. "The best part is that no one will bother me about getting married anymore."

Constance flashed a smile, then her expression went serious again. "Did you hear that Sarah Colby took Orlando a birthday gift?"

I hadn't. "No," I said, wondering why this was significant.

"She's sweet on him, I know it," Constance said, her mouth pulling down at the sides.

Now I understood. I had effectively taken George out of the marriage running for the women in town, and it seemed that Orlando was the main interest now. I didn't know how to console her, so I said, "It will all work out in the end, with the Lord's providence." That put an end to her gossiping.

I finished my purchases, and when I stepped out of the shop, Widow Leeds was just entering with Elizabeth Browne, her neighbor. Elizabeth was a quiet woman, and Widow Leeds more outspoken and friendly—if that was a good descriptor for a nosy woman. I said hello to the women and tried to hurry past, but Widow Leeds grasped my arm. "You're looking well, Susannah."

"Thank you," I said, pulling away from her grasp. She didn't seem to notice my insistence.

"Married life agrees with you," she said, a smile curving her lips, glancing at Elizabeth, who gave an obedient nod. "Should we expect a George Junior in nine months?"

My mouth dropped open, and I couldn't think of how to respond.

Widow Leeds gave a soft laugh. Next to her, Elizabeth smiled. "You're in the circle of married women now, and we can be open about those types of things."

Looking at the widow's wrinkled face and knowing she was older than my own stepmother, I couldn't imagine ever confiding in her about something that happened between George and me. Wasn't there any privacy in this town? I could no longer hold my tongue, and I didn't care if Elizabeth Browne overheard, either. "I don't think my husband would appreciate this conversation," I told Widow

Leeds. "And I'm not a woman to talk behind my own husband's back."

It was Widow Leeds's turn to have her mouth fall open at the statement. I gave her a false smile, then turned away, clutching my purchases, and walked to my horse and cart. Let her spread that bit of news around. Any friends that I might have had would certainly drop me now. I felt Widow Leeds's and Goody Browne's gazes following me as I hurried down the street.

I was grateful I'd come alone because if my mother or father had overheard me, they wouldn't be happy in the least. I might be a married woman of twenty-five, but my parents would have no problem putting me in my place. I couldn't shake the irritation that had crawled up my neck. I'd finally married, satisfied all the speculation that I might turn out to be a true spinster, and now what? They expected me to pop out a child in nine months.

And now, apparently just because I was married, other married women were privy to intimate details about my relationship with George. I'd never had a close friend before, and George had become that, and so much more. I wasn't about to share him, or any information about him, with anyone.

By the time I reached my parents' homestead, I was downright angry. The lone ride and fresh air had done nothing to ease my feelings. When Mother came out to greet me after hearing the arrival of the cart, I handed over her purchase without climbing down. "I'd best get back to George," I told her. "The trip into town took longer than expected."

My mother wasn't one to miss much. "Is everything all right? You look out of sorts."

"I'd just forgotten how nosy everyone is," I said, then slapped the reins on the horse so that it pulled forward.

My mother looked at me with surprise but was wise enough to let me go without pressing for more information. I think she decided it was best for George to get the first earful—one of the benefits of finally marrying me off.

George was nowhere in sight when I pulled up at the house, so I unloaded everything myself and secured the horse in the barn. I went to the main house, and after knocking and entering, I talked to Eve for a few minutes. Hannah was taking a nap, and Eve was nearly napping herself.

"Have you seen George?" I asked her, hoping I didn't sound as desperate as I felt.

Eve only smiled. "He was hammering away not long ago. Maybe he's with your father."

Maybe. Although, I'd have thought my mother would have said something, even when I didn't give her much of a chance.

"Thanks. I'm sure I'll see him soon." I left Eve's side and walked out of the house, then crossed the yard to my small house. Satisfaction coursed through me when I saw all the recent improvements. Tomorrow we'd whitewash, so we'd been spending most of our time sanding everything.

I picked up the supplies from town I'd left on the porch and started to carry them in. The bedroom door was open, and through the doorway, I spotted George sprawled out on the bed. My heart hitched for a moment as I wondered if he'd been injured or was sick, but when his breathing rattled with a snore, I was relieved. But still angry. I'd been through the ringer with the women in town, unloaded the cart myself, took care of the horse, and he was . . . napping?

I set the supplies on the kitchen table and walked into the bedroom and nudged his foot. He jolted awake and turned to look at me. The surprise on his face turned to a smile as he saw me standing there, my arms folded.

"Hello, sweetheart," he said, raspy with sleep.

I narrowed my eyes. "There's nothing sweet about me right now. And the last thing I expected my husband to be doing while I'm facing the gargoyles of Salisbury is to be napping in the middle of the day."

He rolled over and sat up, and at least had the decency to look sheepish. "It's all those nights you've keep me awake and the long days of working in the sun." As if to prove his point, he released a big yawn.

"I'm not the one keeping you awake at night," I said sternly, although inside I was softening.

He reached across the space between us and grabbed my hand and pulled me toward him.

"Hey," I said. "What are you doing?"

"Holding my wife." He tugged me onto his lap, and I landed with an unceremonious thump on him.

"I don't have time to lie in bed all day," I protested.

"We are still newlyweds," George whispered in my ear, pulling me down with him on the bed.

I was tired and cranky, and I knew he would win this battle, so I let myself go limp.

He kissed my cheek, then traced his finger along my neck. "Tell me why you're so upset."

I blinked back the hot burning in my eyes. It all seemed so silly now, but my heart still thumped with indignation. "I was practically drawn and quartered by Widow Leeds."

George's mouth quirked. "That little old woman?"

"There's nothing funny about it," I retorted. "She was with one of her gossipy friends, Goody Browne, and neither of them was interested in being friendly." I told him all that she'd said to me, and instead of getting angry with me, George only laughed.

"She's been a widow for years and is probably trying to

speculate on something more interesting than her dull life." George slid his hands to my waist, pulling me close.

I placed my hand on his chest, keeping him at a distance. "She's going to tell my mother how rude I was," I said, wishing now that I'd been more patient with the woman.

"Let her," George said, clasping my hand on his chest and pulling me closer. "You know, I saw her eyeing me plenty at Meeting. Maybe she was hoping to catch me herself."

I was so startled that I burst out laughing.

George laughed with me, and then leaned down and kissed my neck. "That's better, Susannah. I love to hear you laugh."

I wrapped one arm around his neck, leaning into him and letting my eyes flutter shut. He smelled of sun and work and wood—like a man who spent his days working on his wife's home. "Mmm," I murmured. "That must be it. All the women are jealous of me."

He lifted his head and smiled. "Not as jealous as the men are of me."

I smacked his shoulder. "You're too much. I didn't have one marriage offer before you came along."

George's expression sobered. "That's because I'm the first man you gave a chance to, and even then, I practically had to waylay you after Meeting."

I exhaled, staring into his gray-blue eyes.

"Well, I'm glad you did," I said softly.

His mouth lifted into another smile. "Me, too."

And then he kissed me, and there was no doubt that he didn't intend to go back to his chores for a while. It was nice to be a newlywed, and I found that I didn't mind that I'd found my husband napping in the middle of the day after all.

CHAPTER 29

Salisbury

I WAS PREGNANT. I had to be. My menses cycle was weeks late, and I'd woken up with a sharp stab of nausea spreading from my stomach throughout my body. I'd barely made it to the outhouse before I lost everything I'd eaten the night before, and then some. George had left before the sun rose to start the harvesting. My father was most likely with him, too.

If I could ever get off my knees long enough, I would tell my mother and find out what on this green earth would stop my stomach from churning. Instead, I crouched in the small, stuffy outhouse, feeling like I would pass out if I tried to stand, let alone walk to my parents' home.

Perhaps Eve would miss me when I didn't stop by this morning on my usual rounds. Or maybe little Hannah would come looking for me to tell me something about her doll. She'd finally started to warm up to me over the past couple of weeks when I began sewing new outfits for her dolls.

As it was, I couldn't move, could hardly breathe above the stench. When a voice called my name, I opened my eyes, not knowing how long I'd been in the outhouse.

"Susannah?"

George. It was George. I bolstered as much strength as possible and kicked at the door, pushing it open. It swung shut, and I kicked at it again.

"Susannah!"

He'd seen me. I could hear his footsteps, and moments later, the door opened and his arms were lifting me up.

"What's happened?"

"I—I'm . . ." The strength left me, and it wasn't until George had me inside and I'd had a sip of water that I found my voice again.

"Do you have the stomach illness?"

I shook my head and grasped George's hand. Surely he would be pleased with my news, although I felt fear coursing through me. My body had taken on a mind of its own, and if this was how I felt in the first weeks of pregnancy, how would it be the entire nine months?

"I'm pregnant, George," I said, barely above a whisper.

His eyes widened. "How?" His face reddened. "I mean, how do you know? Are you certain?"

"My menses cycle is late, and I can't stand the thought of food." I pressed a hand against my stomach as another bit of nausea peaked. "I felt ill yesterday morning too, but this morning is infinitely worse."

He pulled me into his arms and laughed. "I can't believe you're pregnant so soon."

"I warned you," I said, feeling a smile start.

George looked again at my face, a myriad of emotions in his expression. "Are you going to be all right?"

"Yes," I said, although I wasn't sure how I knew it. "Many women are ill the first few months of pregnancy. Wasn't Hannah ill, too?"

He shook his head. "Her pregnancies were uneventful . . . until the delivery." A new concern seemed to fill him, and he pulled me against him again, this time so tightly, my breath left me.

"George, I'll be fine," I said, trying to reassure him. I had no idea how my body would manage, but I knew I wanted to bear George's children, and there was only one way to do that.

His fingers threaded through my hair, and he kissed my forehead. "Do you want some bread or some more water? Or something else?"

"Another drink would be nice," I said, suddenly feeling sleepy. "And then I might take a nap."

His brows rose suggestively, and I hurried to say, "Alone. We can't have both of us being idle."

The next weeks continued in a similar pattern, with the mornings being rough, and the afternoons trying to catch up on as many chores as possible. My usual workload exhausted me, and once I told my mother and Eve that I was with child, they began to take on extra work. For Eve, that meant she actually spent more time out of bed than in, and I was impressed at her determination.

By October, I was feeling much better in the mornings, which resulted in more eating. My mother came over to my house on an unusually hot day. "I've had a letter from Mary," she said without preamble and handed it over.

I unfolded the thick piece of paper and read my sister's writing. "Twins? The midwife thinks she's going to have twins?"

"And the pains have been off and on for days," Mother said, pressing her lips together. "Father's back is acting up again, and I dare not leave him alone, especially with you in the family way now."

"I'll go help," I said immediately, not sure where the

thought came from. I hadn't gone to Mary before with her previous births. There was always so much to do at home. And there still was—at my new home—but my sister was having twins.

"George might not like it," my mother pointed out.

"I'll talk to him," I said, feeling confident he wouldn't deny my Christian duty toward my sister, even if it meant that his meals might not be so complete. Eve had rallied somewhat previously, but since I'd started feeling better, she'd become more reclusive again.

"Maybe I can even take Hannah with me," I said, thinking aloud. "She'll get to know her new cousins better, and we can spend time away from Eve and George. I think she'll warm up more." My illness had set our relationship back a step or two.

My mother nodded, although there was a crease between her brows. "I'd be happy to take her, if not." She released a sigh. "Well, go along and talk to George. I can't wait all day."

I wanted to chide my mother for her impatience, but my heart was thumping in anticipation as well. No wonder Mary had seemed so much larger and cumbersome with this pregnancy.

I found George in the barn, and the sight of him pounding out a horseshoe brought new affection for his constant hard work. I showed him my sister's letter, and without me asking, he looked at me, knowledge in his eyes.

"You want to go help her?"

"I do," I said, folding my hands primly in front of me. "I'll take Hannah. She'll think it's a great adventure."

His gaze fell back to the letter in his hands. "How long?"

I lifted my shoulders in a shrug. "A couple of weeks? Until she's able to manage on her own for the most part."

"Hmm," George intoned, not sounding committal one way or another.

"George," I said, stepping closer. "She's having twins, and my mother can't go—you know my father's been ailing again."

"You're pregnant yourself," he said. "What if you get sick again or something else happens?"

I saw the fear in his gray eyes and knew most of it had to do with his first wife's death. She'd died giving birth, though, not in her third month of pregnancy.

"There are doctors in Gloucester, too."

He slid an arm around my waist, and I considered his closeness a good sign. "I'll be a lonely man."

I leaned against him and wrapped my arms about him. "You'll be so busy that you won't notice."

He gave a short laugh. "You think I won't notice my wife missing from my bed?" He pressed a kiss on my cheek, then on my mouth.

"George," I protested halfheartedly as his kiss deepened and his hands roamed.

He smiled and continued to kiss me, until I remembered that my mother was waiting in my kitchen.

"My mother's waiting for our decision," I said, reluctantly pulling away. "She says I can take their cart."

George shook his head. "I'll be driving you to Gloucester, and then I'll return to fetch you back. I don't want anything to happen along the journey."

I reached up and touched the side of his face. "You're a good man, George."

June 2, 1692, Salem Village: At ten o'clock in the jail, a jury of nine women and surgeon John Barton searched the bodies of Rebecca Nurse, Alice Parker, Sarah Good, Elizabeth Proctor, and Susannah Martin for witch marks. They found that Bishop, Proctor, and Nurse each had an odd "excrescense of flesh" on their privates, all strangely alike yet unlike anything natural. But the eldest woman, a skilled midwife, disagreed. The marks looked natural to her, especially after Goody Nurse explained her difficult birthings.

—excerpt from *The Salem Witch Trials*
by Marilynne K. Roach

CHAPTER 30

Salem Jail

AS I WALK OUT of the courtroom, my children surround me. The jailer and guards start to push them back, but then something changes in them, and they allow my children closer. They are all taller than me, grown adults with families of their own. I'm glad they didn't bring my grandchildren with them. I do not want them to see me this way. It's hard enough with my own children.

Richard, John, and Esther come forward first, and I try not to weep as they embrace me. My hands are still tied, so I cannot hold them back. Hannah has also come, George's daughter from his first marriage. There is no difference between her and one of my own. Next, I am in Samuel's arms, then John, Abigail, William, and finally George—my husband's namesake.

Their spouses surround me, and I am overwhelmed. It seems worse than death itself to be pulled away from my loved ones, pulled away from the smallest bit of heaven.

They are gone all too soon, and I am walking through the dank corridor of the jail. Sarah Good rises to her feet as

Rebecca and I enter the cell. Her gaze searches ours, and it's all I can do to shake my head, then collapse in my corner. Rebecca moves more carefully to her place in the cell and kneels down. She clasps her hands in front of her and bows her head. I know she is about to pray, yet I don't want to hear her whispered pleadings.

My own pleadings are silent for now, having formed a hard rock in the center of my chest. I feel as if I've said good-bye to my children for the last time. My fate has been decided, and there is nothing I can do now. I have pleaded not guilty, yet the court has found me guilty.

What sort of miracle would it take for me to taste freedom again? From the moment I stepped into the courtroom, I knew I was ready to fail.

Whatever I've endured today, I know Rebecca Nurse endured worse. To have her hope lit, and then dashed again. Many pleaded for Rebecca in court, yet it was still not enough. I wonder what George would say if he were still alive. More than once he stood up for me in court; he counter-sued. He was always on my side.

My sentence today would have broken his heart. Perhaps he already knows about it and is grieving now.

The women in our cell are quiet. Food is brought, paid for by Rebecca Nurse's family. I eat the hardened bread, if only to stop my stomach from aching. It's not as if I hope to be free of this prison one day and continue on with my life. It feels as if I've spent a lifetime in here.

Little Dorothy climbs on my lap as the sun sets and the prison is cast in a velvety glow. I wrap my arms about her small limbs and close my eyes. Sometimes it's all I can do to breathe in and breathe out. Sometimes that's all I can feel grateful for—air to breathe. It seems it's all I have left now.

Somehow, I sleep through the night, and in the morning

I wake with a throbbing headache and a dry mouth. Dorothy is sleeping next to me, and I move carefully away so as not to disturb her.

Rebecca is kneeling by the cell door, her hands wrapped around the bars. How long has she been there, I do not know, but if she doesn't sleep, she won't live until her execution. The thought should bring a smile of irony with it, but I have no strength for any movement beyond the essential.

"Rebecca," I say, crossing to her and placing my hand on her shoulder. "You need to sleep. The Lord has heard everything you've said already."

Rebecca lifts her head and gazes at me. Her eyes seem unfocused, as if she isn't quite awake. Is it possible to fall asleep while kneeling down?

"Are you all right?" I kneel next to her. Of course she isn't all right, but I hope that my words might bring her some comfort.

"I am seventy-one years old, Goody Martin," she says in a voice that sounds hollow. "I have been a faithful follower of Christ all my life." Her voice breaks, and her mouth trembles.

I tug her hands from the bars and wrap my arms around her. "I know you are devout," I whisper. "And God knows it, too."

CHAPTER 31

Gloucester

THE TOWN OF GLOUCESTER was barely that—perhaps more of a village. I directed George to her home. The outside of the three-bedroom house was well-kept, Puritan fashion, and as we pulled up in the cart, a woman came to the door. I recognized her as Joyce, Mary's neighbor, but I didn't know if it was a good thing she was at Mary's. The woman was a strange bird. Was her presence a sign that Mary had delivered her babies already? Joyce wore an apron, and her hair was pulled back into a bun from her thin face.

Her dark brown eyes made a quick assessment of the new arrivals, and she crossed the yard just as George was helping Hannah and me climb down.

"I thought your mother was coming," she said in a low voice, almost angry.

"My father is ailing," I said, trying to keep my voice patient and steady. I didn't need to get into an argument with this woman moments after arriving in Gloucester. "How's Mary? Has she delivered yet?"

"Soon," Joyce said. "She's been contracting all day. Midwife Hawkes is with her now."

My own stomach tightened as if in response.

Joyce glanced over at George, then to Hannah, who was quietly listening to us. "She's as well as can be expected." Her gaze went back to George. "You're Susannah's husband?"

"Yes, I'm George Martin."

Instead of greeting him, Joyce merely looked back to me. "I hope you've come to help and not rely on my good graces."

I didn't know what to say—at least not anything that would be appropriate in front of Hannah. It was remarkable how the presence of a small, innocent child could curb my tongue. "We've come to help," I said, taking Hannah's hand in mine. "George will be on his way after some refreshment."

"I'll wait out here," George quickly said.

I didn't blame him for wanting to stay out of a house that contained a birthing woman and the likes of Joyce. Hopefully, the midwife would be more pleasant. I followed Joyce inside while Hannah remained with George for a few minutes. Once inside the dim interior, I heard Mary's whimpers coming from the back room.

I immediately pushed the door open and found her in bed with the midwife next to her. My sister's face was pale, and her eyes closed.

"Mary," I said softly and crossed to the side of her bed.

Her blue eyes opened, and a faint smile crossed her face. "You're here." Then she looked past me. "Is Mother coming?"

"It's just me," I said, taking her hand in mine. "Mother is staying to help Father. Joyce tells me that you should deliver today."

"Yes," Mary said faintly, her eyes sliding shut again.

I looked at the midwife, a stocky woman like me, but at least ten years my senior. "How is she?"

Midwife Hawkes gave a small nod. "She's faring well now, but the pains have been slowing down, which isn't good."

I looked back to my sister, but she didn't seem to be aware of what the midwife said. Mary's distended belly looked swollen and painful.

"Where are her other children?"

"Thomas took them into town, and they're going to stay with his mother for a few days."

I thought it wise that the children weren't around for the birth. Now I started to worry about Hannah. She wouldn't have anyone to play with until her new cousins returned.

Thinking of Hannah reminded me that I was going to fetch George something to eat for his return journey. He didn't want to stay overnight and miss a second day of working on our house or helping my father.

I left the bedroom and sliced some bread in the kitchen, then lathered it with Mary's churned butter and took a couple of pieces to George, along with two apples. He and Hannah were in the yard talking to Thomas, who must have just returned.

When Thomas saw me, he said, "Thank you for coming."

I smiled at him—I'd always liked Thomas and thought he was a good husband and father—and handed the food to George. He bent down and kissed me, then was on his way, Hannah clinging to my hand. At least she didn't make a fuss with her father leaving, although I was a bit unsure how she'd fit in with all of her new cousins.

"How is Mary?" Thomas asked me, his brows pulled together in concern.

"She was mostly sleeping," I said, glancing down at Hannah.

Thomas nodded. "I've got to return to the harvest, but if there's any news, come and fetch me." His gaze met mine, and in his gaze, I saw more than what his words might say. He was worried about Mary, just as the midwife was. Delivering twins was not an easy task, no matter the woman.

I took Hannah inside with me and set her to playing with her doll in the kitchen, then went into the back bedroom to check on my sister. Joyce followed, and although I felt uncomfortable with her hovering, it wasn't my place to send her out. Joyce was Mary's neighbor, not mine, and I knew they had a friendship of sorts, even though I'd warned her against it.

Joyce had been ostracized from Meeting the year before, Mary had told me, accused of poisoning another member's cat. Joyce was verbal in her dislike about cats, and when the woman had visited with Joyce, then returned home to find her cat dead, she believed that Joyce had put a hex on the cat.

It was a silly story, but I couldn't discount Joyce's odd ways. Her gaze was piercing, her words direct, and even I, who didn't shy away from being direct myself, felt at odds around her.

Mary's eyes were open when I entered the room, but she didn't seem to be focusing on anything in particular. She was in the bed, not on the birthing chair in the corner, and the midwife hovered over her, pressing a damp cloth against her forehead. The room felt overly warm, and perspiration stood out on both Mary's and the midwife's face.

I knew something wasn't right. I hadn't delivered a child before, but I'd heard many stories, and all of Mary's stories, as well.

"What's going on?" I said quietly to the midwife.

She looked at me, her face unreadable. She glanced at Joyce, and I wondered if the midwife would stay silent with Joyce in the room. But then she said, "Your sister has given up."

I stared at her, stunned. "What do you mean?"

"She's no longer making an effort," Midwife Hawkes said. Her voice trembled as she continued, "It's time to push, but she won't even try."

Everything in my body went cold. "What does that mean? Maybe she needs to rest, and then she can try?"

Joyce moved around the bed to stand on the other side and peer down at Mary. It bothered me she was inspecting my sister so closely, but fear and disbelief were taking over all of my emotions.

"What can we do?" I asked the midwife.

She handed me the cloth and said in a low voice, "I'm going to fetch her husband."

I stared at her. "Is it that serious? There's nothing you can do?"

"I've seen this before," she said, no longer bothering to keep her voice low. "There's nothing more I can do."

I followed her gaze. Mary's eyes were still open, but it was clear she hadn't heard a word we'd said. I took the cloth from the midwife and dipped it into the bowl of water at the bedside, then pressed the cloth against Mary's perspiring brow. There had to be something more. My eyes stung with tears, and my throat swelled as I considered what this might mean for Mary. Was the midwife going to give up, too?

When Midwife Hawkes left, my tears started to fall. Joyce didn't move or speak, and I continued to dab my sister's forehead. Was this really all I could do for Mary?

"Mary," I whispered. Then louder, I said, "Please, Mary. You must try. Don't give up."

Joyce grasped her hand, and I looked over at her. "Have you seen this happen before?" I knew she wasn't a midwife, but she was a couple of decades older than me and certainly had more life experience.

"She stopped drinking the tea I gave her."

I furrowed my brows. "What tea was it?" I didn't really blame my sister for not drinking Joyce's tea, no matter how well-intentioned.

"I fixed her a tea of roots that would help ease her delivery," she said, shaking her head. "Mary complained it made her cramps stronger, and so she refused the second batch I made." Joyce's gaze met mine. "The cramps help prepare the uterus for delivery."

I was silent for a moment. "What's in the tea?"

Although Joyce didn't smile, her eyes brightened. "The mandrake root. I have three different types in my garden, and I've mixed them. I took it with my pregnancies."

I'd had no idea she had children. Were they grown and moved out? "Will it help now?" I asked quietly, not exactly daring to believe I was asking her about a tea that my sister had previously refused.

Joyce gave a shrug. "I don't know, for I never had trouble delivering, you see."

I was curious about her children. Was she a widow? I had never heard about her husband, and I'd never seen a man about her place. Mary's eyes were shut, and her breathing shallow. I wished that the midwife would return and tell me she'd been mistaken. Maybe Thomas could rouse Mary and she'd wake up and try.

"Can you fetch the tea?" I asked Joyce. "We must try something."

Joyce didn't hesitate, but hurried out of the room.

While she was gone, I again spoke to my sister. "Mary,

wake up. You need to deliver these babies. Think of how excited your children will be. Think of Mother and how she'll want to hold them and rock them."

I abandoned the damp cloth and sat next to Mary on the bed. Her extended stomach looked painful, and I placed my hand on her bulge. I couldn't feel the babies moving, but that didn't necessarily mean anything. I found myself praying and pleading that she would be all right, that she'd deliver these children safely.

It seemed ages before Joyce returned, and I was grateful that it was her and not the midwife yet. I didn't know what Midwife Hawkes's reaction would be to the tea.

"I brought a cream that I made as well," Joyce said in a furtive tone. She held out a small jar to me. "Put it under her nose and on her upper chest. It should help her wake up."

Hesitating only a moment, I took the jar and opened the lid. The scent was pungent and sharp, like something soured, but I dug my finger into the jelly-like substance and smoothed it along my sister's upper lip.

Her eyes flew open immediately.

"Mary!" I said, and her eyes slid toward me.

Her mouth opened, but no words came out.

"Put it on her chest too," Joyce said in a hurried voice.

I did as I was told, my fingers trembling, as I prayed that Mary's strength and will would return.

"Drink this, Mary," Joyce said, holding the cup to her lips. The liquid inside steamed, and I hoped it wasn't too hot.

Mary's eyes widened as she gazed at Joyce, and she started to shake her head.

"Please, Mary," I said, taking the cup from Joyce and holding it for Mary.

Her gaze settled on me, and the look of surprise lessened.

"You need to drink this, and then you need to push." I kept my voice firm, even though I was starting to shake and my eyes burned with tears. "Thomas will be here soon, and we want to tell him good news."

"You've done this before, Mary," Joyce added in. "Your body is strong and your mind stronger."

"Come on," I told Mary, wanting to keep her focus on me. "Drink this, and it will help you deliver your babies. They're waiting to see their mother."

Mary lifted her head enough that I was able to get her to sip the liquid. When she tried to push the cup away, I became more adamant. "You have to try, Mary. This tea will give you the strength you need." She drank more, and when she finally relaxed back onto the bed, I was satisfied.

I looked over at Joyce, who gave me a slight nod.

"Mary?" Thomas called out, entering the house.

I moved from the bed, and Joyce and I stood on one side of the room as Thomas entered. He didn't even glance at us but went straight to Mary's side.

"Thomas," she gasped. "The babies are coming."

"They are?" he asked, his voice thick with emotion. "Are you going to be all right?"

"Yes," she said, her face reddening as she let out a cry. "I need to push!"

The midwife that had come in behind Thomas hurried forward. "Let me see her."

Thomas moved back and let the midwife take over. He looked across the room at me, and I nodded. "We'll take care of her. See if Hannah needs anything."

His nod was barely perceptible, but he left the room, and the door shut behind him. I turned back to my sister. Color had flooded her previously pale face, and her listless hands were now clutching the midwife's shoulders as she rose from the bed and sat in the birthing chair.

CHAPTER 32

Gloucester

"TELL ME EXACTLY WHAT was in that tea," I asked Joyce in a hushed voice. Although we were standing at her front door and no one could overhear us, I felt the need to stay quiet. My sister was still in bed with her babies, delivered two days before, healthy and pink. If I hadn't seen Joyce bring in the tea myself, I might have thought a miracle had occurred.

But when Midwife Hawkes saw the remains of the tea in the teacup, she'd chastised both me and Mary, saying that she'd never step foot in Mary's house again. How could I explain that something in the tea had revived Mary and we should be grateful to Joyce? Wasn't Mary's life more valuable than criticizing a disreputable neighbor?

Now, as I gazed at Joyce, insistent in getting answers, she repeated the same herbs she'd told me before. I watched the blue of her eyes carefully. Was it possible to know if someone was telling the truth?

"What else?" I asked, not sure if she was telling me everything, but pretending that I knew she wasn't.

Joyce's gaze shifted away, my first indication that there might be something she wasn't telling me.

"Did you put a spell on it?" I whispered.

Joyce's eyes flew open. "I am not a witch," she hissed. "I did pray over it, just as anyone would pray over a meal. Where's the crime?"

I let her words settle, then I took a measured breath and asked, "What were the words of the prayer?"

She narrowed her gaze. "I don't remember."

Now it was my turn to narrow my gaze. "Try to remember. The midwife is already upset at us and who knows what she'll say to others in town."

Joyce crossed her thin arms over her chest. "I made the tea exactly how I told you, and I didn't cast any spell, in case you think saying a prayer is casting a spell."

Her words stung, yet I had no choice but to believe her. Otherwise I'd have to admit that my sister had delivered her babies through witchcraft.

I turned away from Joyce then, and I felt her watching me all the way back to Mary's house. Inside, I found the children still lingering over their morning meal of porridge. Hannah had made fast friends with her new cousins, which had brought me relief.

The sound of a crying baby came from the back room, and my heart lifted. I would never tire of the sound of a crying baby, alive and healthy, I decided. Hannah looked up at me as I crossed the kitchen, and I patted her head as I walked by her. She ducked her head and smiled. It made me smile, too.

I found Mary in her room just as the crying baby quieted against her breast. She'd had a boy and a girl, so it would be no trouble to tell them apart. Nathaniel and Ruth, she'd named them.

Mary smiled at me as I entered. I picked up little Ruth and held her sleeping form in my arms as Mary held Nathaniel as he suckled. I peered at the infants' dark hair and tiny features. "They are so precious," I said in a reverent tone.

"I have to agree," Mary said. "You've been heaven-sent, Susannah. You must miss George terribly, and Hannah has fit right in with the other children."

I smiled back at her. "I am so grateful that you and the babies are healthy. That's all I could hope for. I've already written to Mother."

Mary nodded. "I think we had our own little miracle."

"Yes," I said, although I was thinking of the tea that Joyce had made. Did Mary even remember drinking it? Surely she'd noticed that the midwife never came back to check on her after the birth. With just the two of us in the bedroom, I had to ask. "Do you remember Joyce being with us when you were delivering?"

Mary's gaze fell to the child in her arms. "I do. She brought over that awful tea again."

I nodded. "When you drank it, everything improved."

Mary looked directly at me. "Do you think it was the tea?"

"What else would it have been?"

"A miracle from God?" Mary asked.

We were both silent for a moment, and then I said, "Possibly. I guess we may never know."

Mary was watching me closely. "You spoke to her, didn't you? That's where you just were? I didn't hear you with the children in the kitchen for the last little while."

I couldn't lie to Mary, not about this. I had too many questions as it was, and I wanted answers. "Yes, I went over and asked Joyce about the ingredients. She said she put in mandrake." I waited for Mary's response.

Finally, she said, "That's not so uncommon. And I know herbs have been used for centuries. But . . ." Her eyes filled with tears. "What if it was something else—what if the miracle of my surviving the birth was not due to the Lord's grace, but because Joyce performed witchcraft?"

The word hung between us in the room like an ugly presence—or even worse, a dark presence with evil intentions. If Joyce had made the tea and cast a spell over the contents, Mary's soul would be owned by the devil himself.

But in this sunny room filled with new life, I couldn't let such dark thoughts overtake me. "Joyce swears she didn't use witchcraft," I said in a whisper.

Mary blinked, and her eyes cleared. "Then we must believe her." She reached out a hand toward me, and I took it, clinging fiercely.

"We both know the tea helped, but we will put our trust that the miracle came from the Lord and not the devil."

Mary nodded vigorously, her eyes bright with unshed tears. "Yes. That is the only way. I can't bear to think that these two innocent children were born healthy due to any other cause."

"Tell me about Joyce's children," I said.

"She has three children, but something happened between her and her husband, and he took them to another town," Mary said in a hushed tone. "She won't speak of it, but gossip says she almost poisoned one of her children. If she did, I don't think it was intentional. There are a few women in Gloucester who don't like her, plain and simple. They'll say any cruel thing about her, true or not."

I let this new information settle, then I asked, "The midwife seemed afraid of her."

Mary nodded. "Midwife Hawkes is part of the group of women. But I don't blame the midwife. She has to always be on the alert with people like Joyce, who give out their advice freely, especially if it contradicts the midwife's."

"Which it did, in your case," I said, although it wasn't necessary.

"Yes," Mary agreed. "Midwife Hawkes can't associate with Joyce because her friends would start ostracizing her if she did."

Our hands remained linked together as Mary's baby continued to suckle until he was sound asleep. Whatever I believed, or whatever evidence lay before me, for Mary's sake, I had to drop my suspicions about Joyce. Speaking against her could only lead to disaster.

The next two weeks raced by as I balanced sanity and sleep and all the children. Fortunately, the twin infants slept a lot, and every time they slept, I demanded Mary rest as well.

I didn't see Joyce, except for an occasional passing in the yard when she was coming or leaving. We didn't speak to each other, apparently by silent mutual agreement. The morning of my departure, I left Mary's house early, before the sun rose, and took a small shovel over to the property line between Joyce's and Mary's home. There I dug up a few of the mandrake roots that Joyce said she'd used in the tea, then I bundled them into a sackcloth, hoping they'd survive the journey back to Salisbury.

A couple of hours later, I was outside with the children when George's wagon came rumbling up the road. My heart thumped as I caught sight of him, and I didn't wait for the wagon to come to a full stop before I was hurrying to him with Hannah at my side. When he climbed down, he scooped up Hannah and hugged her, then he turned to me and gave me a much longer hug.

A warm shiver ran through me at the feel of his breath

on my neck and the beat of his heart against my chest. His arms had never felt so good. When I finally, reluctantly pulled away, he chuckled. "I'm pleased to see you missed me."

I anchored his face with my hands and rose up and kissed him square on the mouth. He prolonged the kiss by pulling me tightly against him.

"Did you miss me?" I whispered, looking into his beautiful gray eyes.

"I missed you more than you'll ever know, Susannah North Martin." George's hands found their way to my waist. "How is George Junior?"

"You mean Esther?"

"A girl name? You would name our son Esther?"

I laughed. "No, we're having a girl."

George leaned down for another kiss. "We'll see, won't we?" His gaze shifted toward the house. "And your sister? Your mother says she fared well and the twins are healthy."

"They are," I said, biting back the other words I could have spoken. I had made a pact with Mary. What happened during the delivery would stay between the two of us, and hopefully the midwife would also keep her mouth shut. I hugged George again, feeling so relieved he was here. I'd loved spending time with my sister and her family, but I was more than ready to go home.

"And how are you feeling?" George said, tilting my chin up so our gazes met.

"The worst seems to be over," I said. "Or maybe I haven't had time to feel sick. Once I'm back home, I'll stay in bed all day and you can rub my feet."

One side of George's mouth lifted, which only made me want to kiss him again. "That would be a pleasure, my wife."

June 2, 1692, Salem Village: At four o'clock, the same committee of one male surgeon and nine matrons examined Bridget Bishop, Rebecca Nurse, Elizabeth Proctor, and Susanna Martin. The obvious excrescences of the morning were not to be found, only a bit of dried skin where some had been observed. Furthermore, Goody Martin's breasts, full and firm at ten o'clock, were now "all lank and pendant."

—excerpt from *The Salem Witch Trials*
by Marilynne K. Roach

CHAPTER 33

Salem Jail

IT HAS BEEN LESS than a day since my trial, and now Elizabeth Howe and Sarah Wildes will stand before the afflicted girls. I wait for their return, pacing the cell, back and forth and around. Back and forth again, stopping at each wall, then stopping at the row of bars reaching from floor to the cragged ceiling.

The sun arcs in the sky, then begins its western trek. Soon, I know, the women will return. And soon, we'll know the fate of the two remaining women in our cell.

Rebecca Nurse has prayed her last, it seems. She is quiet as she sits against the wall, her knees pulled up to her chest, her head bowed over her arms. Sarah Good is quiet too. She spent part of the morning teaching Dorothy her letters using a stick to carve in the filth of the floor. It's the most animated I've seen Sarah since the death of her baby.

Dorothy is eager at first, but her hunger and exhaustion take over after a while, and her mother falls silent, too.

Finally, there are footsteps and voices. I turn, watching for the first appearance of Elizabeth or Sarah Wildes.

They both come into view nearly at the same moment, and the jailer unlocks the cell door and lets them inside. I look for any sign in their eyes. What has happened? What is the verdict?

I turn to Sarah Wildes, but she simply covers her face with her hands and sinks to the floor. My heart stutters. I look to Elizabeth for answers. But she has turned away from me, back toward the bars, gripping them with her hands. A moment later, I see why. Her daughter has led her husband to the cell, and although he cannot see her, I can see the love in his expression for his wife. Almost desperately, Elizabeth clasps his hands in hers. They whisper together for a long time, and I want to turn away, to leave my place, in order to give them their privacy. Oh, how they must be grieving.

George has already left this earth, and I wonder what it would have been like if I had known in advance of his death. What might have our last words been together?

When Elizabeth's husband shuffles away, led by their tearful daughter, I want to sink to my own knees and weep. But I no longer have tears left.

I am surprised when Elizabeth turns toward us, her chin lifted, her eyes clear. "The moment I walked into that courtroom, the afflicted started to act up. They said they could not even bear to look at me." She shakes her head, but still her voice is strong. "They swooned and had seizures, despite the fact that a dozen people testified on my behalf."

Now, her voice breaks as she continues, "Even my ninety-four-year-old father-in-law was there. At his age, why should he be compelled to stand as a witness in a witch trial? Where is the justice in that?"

Sarah Wildes rises to her feet, her hair tugged free of its braid. "The ministers of Rowley even testified on Elizabeth's behalf. Samuel Phillips and Edward Payson defended her against the Perley family accusations. Phillips even said that he'd overheard the Perley girl's brother try to get her to call Elizabeth a witch."

Elizabeth nods at this. "I was blamed for dead cattle, sick children, weary horses, rotten fence posts, and trampled fields. It seems that all of those random events made the testimonies of the others obsolete."

"And she was found guilty of witchcraft," Sarah Wildes continues. "And so was I."

We all stare at her. It is as we all believed, but Sarah Wildes seems to have come undone. She no longer cares who might overhear or who might testify against her. She has been found guilty, and there is no longer any recourse.

"My husband's first wife's family testified against me. They were more than happy to see me sentenced," Sarah Wildes says. "Their accusations were nothing new, and they were eager to share their long-standing suspicions with the court today." She takes a shaky breath.

Elizabeth fills in for her, and it's as if they lived through the same trial, side by side. "Her son, Ephraim, stopped courting the Symmonds girl when her family sided against Sarah. She was also blamed by the Andrews brothers for a destroyed wagon full of hay when they borrowed her scythe."

"And so what if their hay was ruined?" Sarah Wildes asked. "Do I deserve to hang for that? Their sister, Elizabeth, said that a cat walked across her that night—which, of course, was me since she didn't own a cat."

Elizabeth gives a bitter laugh. "She was also blamed for when Mary Reddington fell off her horse into a brook."

I am shaking my head at the ridiculous accusations by so many, but mostly I am trembling with disbelief and anger.

I cross to Sarah and reach out my hand. She grasps it and squeezes, then she is in my arms. "Guilty, they said. I am found guilty."

I close my eyes and hold her as she cries. We have spent weeks together in hell, and it isn't getting any better. But we have stopped expecting anything better. It seems that even God has gone silent.

Chapter 34

Salisbury

THE HEAT OF THE days had finally dissipated, and although the harvest was in, there was still much to do on the farm. George spent part of each week in town, working for the blacksmith, to hone his skills and earn a faster income. When he was home, he worked on building the second room onto our house for the baby. He also said that he wanted Hannah to move in with us as soon as the bedroom was finished. That would give her some time to get used to living with George and me in a family unit before the baby came.

Hannah was excited about her new bedroom, but she still spent most of her time with Eve. With autumn in full force, the leaves had changed their green to orange, yellow, and red, creating a lovely tapestry throughout all of Salisbury.

My belly had grown, but I felt strong and healthy, and my appetite was more than healthy. I was eating nearly as much as George now, and he laughed every time about it. Today, he was in town, and Hannah and I were on our own as Eve took an afternoon nap.

"Come help me with the rugs, Hannah," I said, finding her playing with her dolls in the kitchen. Apparently, they were having their supper early, and Hannah had set out plates and saucers for each doll.

"Can I borrow your mistress for a moment, ladies?" I said to the dolls, looking at each one in turn as if they were real people.

Hannah let out a small giggle.

"Thank you very much," I continued, speaking to the dolls. Then I turned to Hannah. "I guess you are free now. Can you bring the rug out from the bedroom?"

We hung the rugs over the outside porch rail, and I watched as Hannah enthusiastically beat the rugs with a wooden paddle. It was perhaps her favorite chore.

"Susannah," my mother's voice interrupted.

I looked over to see her approaching the house. She was out of breath and must have hurried across the fallow fields. In her hand, she gripped a letter.

"What is it?" I asked, not liking her pale complexion. I grasped Hannah's arm to keep her from beating the rugs, and in the new silence, I asked, "Is it Mary? Or the babies? Or Sarah?"

"No," my mother said. Her gaze flitted to Hannah. "I need to speak to you, inside."

I understood her meaning and told Hannah to continue with the rugs, that I needed to go inside for a moment.

Once in the kitchen, my mother sat down heavily on a chair and slid the letter across the table, but kept her hand over it so that I couldn't pick it up yet. "Widow Leeds came over a few days ago, and as usual she filled me in on the town gossip."

I furrowed my brow, not sure what this all had to do with me.

"She told me about a letter that she received from Midwife Hawkes in Gloucester," my mother continued.

My head started to pound. I knew this could not be good news. If Widow Leeds, who already disliked me, was friends with the Gloucester midwife, then communication between them would never favor me.

"I didn't believe her claims, and so she brought the letter to me today," my mother said, holding up the envelope. Her eyes narrowed as she watched my reaction. "Are the midwife's claims true, Susannah? Did you let Mary's neighbor Joyce perform witchcraft in Mary's home?"

I pulled the letter from my mother's hand and opened it. My eyes fell on the scrawled words, and my heart lodged in my throat as I read the terrible lies that the midwife had written to Widow Leeds.

Meeting my mother's gaze, I said, "Joyce brought over a tea to give to Mary. She drank a little of it, but the tea was similar to what we use in Salisbury, made of mandrake. It was through prayer and faith that her delivery went well, not through witchcraft."

The air between my mother and me was absolutely still and silent.

"What else was in the tea?" my mother asked, trembling.

"I spoke to Joyce on more than one occasion, and she denied any spells or hexes." I felt confident in telling my mother this, but inside, I had doubted myself. It had been easy to forget about when I was no longer in Gloucester to be confronted with the reminder.

"You know that Widow Leeds won't let this rest," my mother said, her expression becoming pinched.

"I will speak with her," I said, dreading it, but knowing that I must. "She cannot bring these rumors to Salisbury.

And I need to know who else Midwife Hawkes might have spoken to." I wondered if I should write to Mary or try to take care of it all myself.

"You can't go to every town and confront the gossipers," my mother said.

I reached for the shawl hanging by the door, and said, "Can you watch out for Hannah until Eve wakes up from her nap? And if George returns before me, tell him I'll be back before dark."

My mother stood. "Susannah, let's think about this."

I held up the letter. "I've had plenty of time to think about this already. It's time for me to speak to Widow Leeds." I pulled the shawl about my shoulders. "As distasteful as confronting Widow Leeds will be, I'll do anything to protect Mary."

My mother gave a short nod and, surprisingly, didn't try to stop me again. She grasped my hand before I left. "Take care."

It wasn't a casual endearment, but more of a warning. I opened the door, told Hannah to mind her grandmother, and I set off, cutting across the fields to save me time. I wanted to be home before dark. I might even be able to ride back with George if I was quick enough. But I also knew that I wouldn't hurry my time with Widow Leeds. She absolutely had to understand every word I'd speak to her.

The lane that led to Widow Leeds's home was overgrown with thick weeds that were now half dead. I supposed that the woman didn't own a horse and cart, or if she did, rarely used it. She probably found that unnecessary since she was only a short distance from town, and she was still a spry woman, easily able to walk to my mother's place and others throughout the area for visiting and gossiping.

Her two-bedroom house was in need of a good

whitewash, and her yard was as unkempt as the road. I almost felt compassion for her in her lonely, widowed state. I knew that her only child, a son, rarely came to visit. The condition of the outside of her home was testament to that.

But when I knocked and the door swung open with a soft creak, I saw that the interior of her home was spotless, more in keeping with our Puritan standards.

Widow Leeds's deep-set eyes nearly popped out when she saw me standing on her threshold. Her mouth opened, then closed, and opened again when I lifted the letter I held in my hands. "Good afternoon," I said. "I've come to speak with you about a private matter."

She didn't move for a moment, but then I could tell she was aware of the possibility of a neighbor seeing me standing on her doorstep, and she had to weigh her decision. Finally, she stepped back, holding the door open, and I slipped inside.

The interior was brighter than I might have imagined. A glass jar of late wildflowers sat on the scrubbed kitchen table, and beyond the room, I could see partially into her bedroom. Her bed was covered with a yellow-and-blue quilt, neatly cornered at the edges. Widow Leeds might not have much in the way of a yard, but the inside of her home was immaculate.

She led me to a set of chairs, one upholstered and the other a rocking chair, which were arranged near the hearth. The fire in the fireplace was weak, but the room was remarkably warm. I realized I couldn't hear the wind that had kicked up a short time ago. This small home had been well-built. I took the upholstered chair myself and waited as she sat in the rocking chair.

And then, without any preamble, I opened the letter and began to read.

As I read, Widow Leeds clenched her hands in her lap—the only indication I knew she was listening. For she was barely breathing, and she made no comment as I repeated the midwife's poisonous words against me and my sister Mary.

When I finished, the silence stretched between us. And when I spoke, she would not meet my eyes. "Your friend Midwife Hawkes is making a false accusation," I said. "I would have never allowed Joyce to give my sister something made through witchcraft. Mary's delivery was difficult, and it was only through the Lord's blessing that she and her two babies fared well. I will not give any credit to the devil."

My words were simple, but the tone of my voice fiery. When Widow Leeds did meet my gaze, I saw that her eyes were equally hard.

"You will not spread malicious rumors about my sister," I said in a harsh whisper, "and if you do, you will regret every single day of your life until you die." With Widow Leeds staring at me in contempt, I slowly ripped the letter in half, then into quarters, and then into eighths. As she watched, I fed the pieces of the letter into her fire.

The weak flames rallied around the new fuel and sprang to life as it curled, then singed, and finally burned the letter in its entirety.

As we both watched the smoke rise from the black ashes of the letter, Widow Leeds finally spoke. "I will not bring shame to your sister's name," she said. "But I will make sure you regret my acquaintance."

The breath left me then, for I knew that Widow Leeds had more friends and connections in Salisbury than me. She had influence where I did not. The docile bones in my body were few. And Widow Leeds would, I knew, use that to her full advantage.

As I left her home, I saw her neighbor, Elizabeth Browne, hurry inside her house. I had the sense that the woman had been trying to figure out what was going on at Widow Leeds's home, and now the last person Elizabeth wanted to speak with was me.

But I could take whatever she sent my way. Mary would be protected, I sensed that clearly. In Mary's stead, I would take whatever ridicule Widow Leeds came up with. I just hoped that it wouldn't extend to my family, my George, my Hannah, or my unborn child.

PETITION FOR REBECCA NURSE

Samuel Aborn Jr.
Daniel Andrews
Sarah Andrews
Edward Bishop Sr.
Hannah Bishop
Peter Cloyse
Elizabeth Cook
Isaac Cook
Samuel Endicott
Nathaniel Felton Sr.
Joseph Holton Sr.
Joseph Holton Jr.
Joseph Hutchinson
Lydia Hutchinson
Sarah Leach
Hannah Osborne
William Osborne
Margaret Philips
Tabitha Phillips
Walter Phillips Sr.
Elizabeth Porter
Israel Porter
Benjamin Putnam
Jonathan Putnam
Joseph Putnam
Lydia Putnam
Rebecca Putnam
Sarah Putnam

Daniel Rea
Hepzibah Rea
Joshua Rea
Sarah Rea
Samuel Sibley
Esther Swinnerton
Job Swinnerton

—*The Salem Witch Trials* by Marilynne K. Roach

CHAPTER 35

Salem Jail

THE DAYS GROW HOTTER as July descends upon us. We spend our time mostly sitting, sometimes talking, but always in a state of numbness. News of other trials filters into our little cell in our corner of the world. We hear of accusations against Dorcas Hoar as she stands trial in the Salem Courthouse.

Ann Pudeator is questioned a second time in Beadle's Tavern. A woman by the name of Sarah Churchill tells of how Ann's specter asked her to sign the Devil's book. When faced with the direct accusation, Ann's response is what all of ours would have been: "I never saw the Devil's book nor knew he had one."

When will this madness end? With all of our deaths? Will that be enough? Will they continue until there is no one left alive and the accusers turn on each other? As the reports of accusations, and those who are being tried, trickles in, we are not surprised at any of it. We have heard accusations even beyond our own imaginings.

Mary Bradbury is not only accused by the afflicted girls, but by the ghost of her uncle. The girls say they saw John Carr's spirit appear in the courtroom and claim that Mary murdered him.

My mind spins at the implausibility of it all, yet the craze continues.

Rebecca Nurse has gone back to praying, and it is Sunday, July 3, when she has a visitor to our cell. It's an elder from her church's congregation. She rises to her feet in surprise to greet the elder, and the jailer lets her out of the cell.

The elder's voice is stiff as he says, "Come with me. You've been asked to appear at the Meeting House."

I watch the jailer lead her away and wonder what she was possibly needed for. My mind turns over the possibilities, but I can't come up with anything satisfying. When Rebecca returns, she hasn't been gone all that long, yet her coloring is paler than usual.

She nearly stumbles into the cell. Elizabeth and I rush to her and grasp her arms.

"What happened?" I ask as the jailer moves away down the corridor.

She blinks at me, as if just realizing that I am there holding her arm.

"Reverend Nicholas Noyes asked me to stand before the elders, and then he made a list of my sins and offenses." Rebecca's eyes fill with tears that tumble onto her papery cheeks. "He declared on behalf of the church that I am spiritually unclean."

This. This is more painful than a sentence of death. I can feel Rebecca's heart twisting in grief and disbelief as if it were my own. "No," I say, not quite comprehending.

"I have been excommunicated." Her voice is dull and lifeless.

I can only stare at her. Next to us, Elizabeth rests her head on Rebecca's shoulder. "The Lord knows your heart," she whispers.

Is it possible that an entire congregation could turn on their most devout member? Today it is possible.

We are stunned. We are helpless.

The following day, on Monday, Rebecca's family and neighbors put together a petition, and thirty-nine people sign it. Rebecca writes her own statement about what she meant when she referred to Goody Hobbs, not as fellow witches, but as fellow prisoners.

I look over her shoulder as she writes in her careful script: "And I being something hard of hearing, and full of grief, none informing me how the court took up my words, and therefore had not opportunity to declare what I intended, when I said they were of our company."

Late in the evening, we hear back. Thomas Fisk, the jury foreman, has also written a statement explaining the reversal of Rebecca's verdict. Rebecca's family took all of the documentation to Boston and handed it to Governor Phips.

After considering the petitions and statements, Phips grants Rebecca a reprieve.

Is this God's miracle? Can we trust in it?

I do not even care about the reports coming in about how the afflicted are tortured again when they hear about the reprieve. All I know is that perhaps good really will outweigh evil, and not in the way the magistrate and jurors think.

There is a small bit of hope for one of us.

We wait and we start praying again.

If there is a reversal for Rebecca, that might mean a change for the rest of us. If the petition of thirty-nine people can overpower the accusations of a handful of young girls, then perhaps there is justice in Salem.

And then the word comes. An unnamed man from Salem has persuaded Governor Phips to revoke his order. There is no longer a reprieve for Rebecca Nurse. She will hang with the rest of us.

CHAPTER 36

Salisbury

GEORGE CAME INTO THE kitchen, a letter clutched in his hand, his face pale. It had been a full week since my visit with Widow Leeds, and although I'd expected this day to arrive, when it did, fear gripped me as never before. What had she done? What had I done?

"Susannah," George said, and it was in that single word that I knew I had much to fear.

"What?" I whispered, for my voice had fled completely. I'd told George about my visit with Widow Leeds and what had truly happened in Gloucester with Joyce and Mary. I had to. It was the only way I could reclaim a full night's sleep. Yet I still hadn't slept well after my visit with Widow Leeds.

"The reverend is coming tonight to our home to discuss an accusation made against you."

My body numbed, and my hands went cold. I reached for the letter, and George released it into my hands. The note was brief, stating that an accusation had been made against me by a member of our congregation. I exhaled, knowing it was Widow Leeds. Had she condemned my sister then? If so, why was I the one being visited by the reverend and not my parents? Unless this extended to them as well.

I looked up at George, seeing the fear in his eyes mirroring my own. "Susannah," he said again, his voice softer, searching. I stood and fell into his arms and let him hold my awkwardly expanded body against him. "I won't let anything happen to you," he said, and for the moment, I let myself believe him. I didn't think I could make it through the next few hours without that belief.

George sent Hannah to the main house to stay with Eve while the reverend visited. When the reverend pulled up on his horse, without his cart or his wife with him, I knew that I could no longer deny the seriousness of what was about to transpire. This was no social call.

I'd laid out tea and fresh bread, the baking of which had at least kept my hands busy that afternoon, although my mind continued to be tormented by speculation and unanswered questions. It was only George's steadying presence that kept me from running out of the house as far as I could until I collapsed in exhaustion. The worry and strife couldn't be good for my unborn child either, and that was why I'd forced myself to breathe and carry on with my usual tasks.

At the sound of the approaching horse coming from outside, George looked at me from across the room where he'd just stoked the fire. Our gazes said everything our words did not. We were both on edge; we were both afraid.

When the reverend knocked softly on the door, it was George who crossed the room to open it. I stayed in the corner of the kitchen, clutching at the apron tied about my waist, as if I were a small child and the apron was a comfort blanket.

"Mr. Martin," the reverend said, his gaze scanning the room until it landed on me. "Goody Martin."

"Welcome to our home," George said. "Please, come sit by the fire. Susannah has prepared some refreshment."

The reverend hesitated for the slightest moment, and I worried that he might refuse our hospitality. After all, he hadn't come here with pleasing news. But when he followed George's directive and sat in the armchair by the hearth, I breathed easier.

I turned from the men then and prepared a tray of cups of tea and slices of buttered bread, all the while my hands trembled. By the time I served the men, they were in quiet conversation about how the people of Salisbury had fared during harvest season. I wished that the conversation could have continued indefinitely, and that the reverend's presence in our home was nothing but a social visit, but I knew he was only biding his time.

Finally, tea half drunk, and with me sitting next to George, both of us across from the reverend, he set down his cup deliberately and raised his gaze to me. He reached into his vest pocket and pulled out a folded piece of paper, but instead of opening it and reading whatever charges lay within, he said, "An accusation has been made against you, Goody Martin. The accusation is serious, indeed, and as the reverend of our congregation, it is my duty to proceed with the appropriate action."

My mouth opened, but there was not a word I could say that would redeem me without knowing what accusation he was speaking of. I dared not give him any more information than what he might need to know.

"Widow Leeds has claimed that you visited her a week ago yesterday."

My breath stalled. So it had happened. Just as I knew it would.

"She says that you had a disagreement, that you had turned your nose up at her when she asked after your family," the reverend continued.

I stole a quick glance at George, who was intently listening to the reverend. My heart and stomach were sinking together equally fast.

"She says that you have been ill-mannered toward her in the past, and when you left last week, her cat died the same night."

My eyes widened. I hadn't heard of her cat dying. Surely the gossip would have reached at least my mother. Regardless, I hadn't even noticed her cat that day. I found myself leaning forward slightly, wanting to hear every word and nuance of what the reverend was saying.

It was his turn to take a deep breath, and for a moment I pitied him in his role—to solve a dispute between two headstrong women. "Widow Leeds claims that you cursed her cat, that you've never liked her cat, and out of spite you wished the animal dead."

I stared at the reverend, and he had no trouble staring back. I waited for a long moment, for him to continue, for him to tell me of Widow Leeds's other accusations about Joyce and her witchcraft and how I allowed her to give my sister the devil's tea. But the reverend had been silent for so long, watching me, that I realized there were no more accusations.

"That is all?" I asked, trying to keep the triumph and relief out of my voice. I didn't want to appear insolent, lest it led him to presume my guilt.

One of his brows lifted, but he only said, "That is her entire accusation. What do you have to answer for yourself?"

I wanted to laugh, but I knew it would only cause concern for both my husband and the reverend. A dead cat was all that Widow Leeds could come up with? Is this her vengeance? Even though the accusation was false, at least it was better than what she could have said. Yet, the fact that she did make an accusation against me meant that she was a determined woman of her word.

"I did not even see her cat the day we spoke," I said. "And I have no particular issue with cats, or any animals. Who is her witness?" I folded my hands in my lap lest their trembling should give away my angst. For it was building up inside me quicker than I could tamp it down.

"Elizabeth Browne."

Of course.

"Do you deny the accusations?" he asked.

"I do."

"Would you be willing to testify in court?" the reverend asked.

George shifted forward, propping his elbows on his knees. "What are the benefits of a court proceeding in a case like this?"

The reverend looked over at him. "Goody Martin will have an opportunity to defend the accusations in a public setting."

My stomach knotted at the thought of standing before a magistrate and his judges—and whoever else in town came to the hearing—and refuting Widow Leeds's accusations.

"And if she does not take this to court, what will the consequences be?" George asked.

I could see where he was leading with this line of questioning. He wanted everything to be forgotten and put into the past. He wanted to protect Mary as well. Would going to court just stir up Widow Leeds even more?

The reverend's steady gaze was back on me. "You will pay a fine of twenty shillings, and we would move your Meeting seat placement farther back in the congregation."

My breath stilled. Relocating my family bench meant that everyone in the congregation would find out what had happened. It would be a public humiliation, to say the least. And most likely, my family would join me, bringing condemnation to us all.

"That's unreasonable," George said. "Susannah's family has been a part of this town for many years, and they are a respected family. To move Susannah would affect all of her family members. Think of her mother and father. Think of her married sisters."

It was exactly what I was thinking of—my married sister and her family.

"Mr. Martin, I've already considered all the ramifications. Widow Leeds's accusation is not to be taken lightly, and this sentence will satisfy her and will offer redemption to your wife."

I looked over at George and saw the emotions moving across his face. He stood and paced the room, and the reverend sat back, unaffected by George's posturing. If I went to court, this minor accusation had the potential to escalate into something that none of us wanted. I could bear the public speculation and shame for a short time.

"George," I said softly, standing to stop him from pacing. I placed a hand on his arm. "We will pay the fine, and I will take the seat placement. You and Hannah will remain with my family." I turned to the reverend. "How long will I have to sit farther back in the congregation?"

"Six months," he said.

"But the baby will come before then," George said, but I could see that he'd become convinced by my plea.

"It is not so very long," I said, looking George in the eye. He had to understand what it meant to me to keep my sister safe and to keep other rumors from surfacing. Being accused of cursing a cat was something I could live with.

George gazed at me, the depths of his eyes intent on mine, as if to ask me if I was sure.

I gave him a nod, too small for the reverend to notice. When George turned to speak to the reverend, I already knew the answer he gave.

"We will pay the fine, and I will sit with Susannah at Meeting until her probation is finished."

The reverend bowed his head and then gripped George's hand. The decision had been agreed on, and now it would just take living with. I didn't look forward to telling my parents, and then explaining to Eve and Hannah why I wouldn't be sitting on the family bench with them at Meeting.

Thankfully, Hannah wasn't in school yet and wouldn't be faced with teasing by any children. When the reverend left our home in the darkness of the night, I fell into George's arms and let the tears come.

He held me tightly against his strong chest and surrounded me with the sense of security that only his arms could provide. Mary was safe. At least for now. I'd keep my head up and pay the penance that the reverend had declared and watch Widow Leeds gloat from a distance. But I wouldn't let myself care.

"I need to tell my parents tonight or I'll never sleep."

George pulled away, and I could see in his eyes that he knew it was futile to argue with me. "All right, I'll come with you."

We left our house and set off across the field, hand in hand, walking beneath the moonlight. It felt good to have George by my side in this. And even though my stubborn heart was pounding, I told myself that, with George, everything would be all right. We were together, we were married, and we were expecting our first child. Our life wasn't perfect, but we would face it together.

My mother did not take the news well—not that I expected her to. My father was stoic and quiet, but I could see the concern in his eyes.

"Susannah," my mother said when George and my father were speaking in quiet tones to each other. "How many times have I told you to curb your tongue? You should have never gone to confront Widow Leeds."

"I did it for Mary," I whispered. "You know that. This accusation is much more lenient than what she could have accused me, or Mary, of."

"Yes, but you will be publicly humiliated," my mother said, her eyes filling with tears.

I grasped her hand, feeling my own eyes burn with emotion. "It will soon pass," I told her, trying to convince her as well as myself.

CHAPTER 37

Salisbury

THE REVEREND HADN'T WASTED any time in enacting my punishment. The very next Sabbath, I was assigned my new seat placement. Widow Leeds sat three rows in front of me, and my parents were two rows in front of her. George sat by me as he'd promised, but I'd told Eve to take Hannah to my parents' bench. There was no reason for all of us to suffer, although it wouldn't stop the gossip.

During the break between meetings, I felt Widow Leeds's eyes on me as she stood with a group of ladies, including Elizabeth Browne, most likely talking about me. She'd greeted my mother, but said nothing to me. By the end of the afternoon, the entire congregation would be filled in on my misdeeds.

When Meeting had concluded and we were on our way back home, George and I up front in the cart, and Eve riding in the back with Hannah, I realized that the only people I'd talked to that afternoon had been my own family members. I had perhaps never felt a particularly close part of the community, but the people of Salisbury were still my people, and now I had been singled out as different.

I released a sigh without knowing it had been audible.

George reached for my hand and grasped it, whispering, "I can speak with the reverend again."

"No," I said, squeezing his hand, grateful for his comfort. "Let it be." My words were stronger than the turmoil that churned inside of me. The months would pass swiftly, I told myself, and things would return to normal. Perhaps not with Widow Leeds or Elizabeth Browne, but they'd never been friends to me in the first place. "Do you think Hannah was teased at Meeting?"

George glanced back at her, then shook his head. "I didn't see her around any children."

That may or may not have been a good thing. My hand rested on my growing belly. How would my child fare in a town such as Salisbury?

When we arrived home, I started supper preparations while Hannah went to the main house with Eve. With George feeding the horse in the barn, I walked outside to my little garden plot. I wouldn't be planting anything until the spring in the tilled earth, but I'd buried the mandrake roots that I'd dug up from Joyce's garden. I hoped they would survive the winter and grow in the spring, in time for my own delivery.

I didn't know how those roots saved my sister's life, but they did, and witchcraft or not, I wasn't going to risk delivery complications. I planned to make my own tea in the spring, and by the time my delivery day came, I'd be strong and capable, just as Joyce had been, and just as Mary too.

This was one thing I hadn't shared with George, and I intended to keep it that way.

CHAPTER 38

Salem Courthouse

Warrant for Executions
Signed by William Stoughton July 12, 1692

To: To Georg: Corwine Gent'n High Sheriff of the County of Essex Greeting

Whereas Sarah Good Wife of William Good of Salem Village Rebecka Nurse wife of Francis Nurse of Salem Villiage Susanna Martin of Amesbury Widow Elizabeth Howe wife of James How of Ipswich Sarah Wild Wife of John Wild of Topsfield all of the County of Essex in their Maj'ts Province of the Massachusetts Bay in New England Att A Court of Oyer & Terminer held by Adjournment for Our Soveraign Lord & Lady King William & Queen Mary for the said County of Essex at Salem in the s'd County on the 29th day of June [torn] were Severaly arraigned on Several Indictments for the horrible Crime of Witchcraft by them practised & Committed On Severall persons and pleading not guilty did for their Tryall put themselves on God & Thier

Countrey whereupon they were Each of them found & brought in Guilty by the Jury that passed On them according to their respective Indictments and Sentence of death did then pass upon them as the Law directs Execution whereof yet remains to be done:

Those are Therefore in their Maj'ties name William & Mary now King & Queen over England &ca: to will & Comand you that upon Tuesday next being the 19th day of [torn] Instant July between the houres of Eight & [torn] in [torn] forenoon the same day you Elizabeth Howe & Sarah Wild From their Maj'ties Goal in Salem afores'd to the place of Execution & there Cause them & Every of them to be hanged by the Neck untill they be dead and of the doings herein make return to the Clerke of the said Court & this precept and hereof you are not to fail at your perill and this Shall be your Sufficient Warrant Given under my hand & seale at Boston the 12'th day of July in the fourth year of the Reign of our Soveraigne Lord & Lady Wm & Mary King and Queen &ca:

—*Wm Stoughton*
Annoq Dom. 1692

[Reverse side of warrant]

Salem July 19th 1692

I caused the within mentioned persons to be Executed according to the Tenour of the with [in] warrant.

—*George Corwin Sherif*

CHAPTER 39

Salisbury

MY SON MADE HIS entrance into the world with a whimpering cry on June 29. George didn't even wait for my mother to tell him that he could enter the bedroom, and suddenly he was there, at my side, looking down at the tiny infant with a head full of black hair.

"Hello, Richard," George said. We'd chosen names over the past few weeks—Richard if the baby was a boy, and Esther if she was a girl.

Despite my exhaustion, I smiled at my husband's attention to our son. My child had been born healthy, and next week, my seat replacement would be reinstated at Meeting. Widow Leeds and her neighbor Elizabeth Browne still didn't speak to me, and they were barely cordial to my mother. I didn't need their friendship anyway. George and my little family were all the happiness I needed.

Hannah came into the bedroom next, and she was sweet to baby Richard, petting the top of his head as one would a family pet.

The room filled from there with my parents and Eve, and amid all the exclamations and congratulations, I continued to smile. I could sleep later. Then still later, I would throw out the remains of the mandrake tea I'd been drinking over the past month—the same concoction that Joyce had told Mary would help her have an easy delivery.

It would be my own secret. There had been no witchcraft performed, no spells spoken, only common sense in making a healthy tea out of mandrake roots.

"He's beautiful like his mother," George said, leaning down and kissing my brow.

I hadn't noticed until now, but it was only the two of us in the room. The midwife had gone to clean up, and I could hear the voices of my family coming from the kitchen, likely preparing a meal.

"I think he looks like you," I said. Even in the reddened baby face of my new son, I could see George's features. I marveled at the tiny, perfect result that came from the union between a man and woman.

George gave an indulgent laugh. "That might not be a good thing. Hopefully, he'll favor you more as he gets older."

I grasped his hand, feeling an urgency to speak my mind. "George," I said, and his gray eyes met mine. He looked tired, although his gray eyes were the color of a promising morning. We'd all had a sleepless night as my labor had extended hour after hour. "Have I ever said *thank you* for asking me to marry you?"

George settled gently on the bed next to me and lowered his face until I could feel his breath upon my face. "I couldn't help it, you know. You're the most beautiful woman in Salisbury, and the fact that you were single was truly a miracle."

I wanted to swat his arm, but I didn't have the energy.

Instead, I settled for a smile and a lift of my eyebrows. I knew at that moment I looked far from attractive. My hair was damp with perspiration, and my skin sagged with the weight gained during pregnancy. "You are a fool, George," I teased.

"A smitten fool, then," he said in a lowered voice.

"How can you compliment me?" I asked. "I'm hardly fit to even look at."

His fingers moved to my hairline as he smoothed back the tendrils. Then he kissed me—truly kissed me with a passion that I was grateful my parents weren't in the room to witness. When he lifted his head, and I made an effort to catch my breath, he said, "We'll always be together, Susannah. You, me, Hannah, Richard, and our children."

My hand clung to his, and I believed him with all my heart. In my arms, little Richard Martin stirred with a small cry. I smiled at the miniature of my husband. It was time to turn my attention to my baby and start raising my family.

Sarah Good stood at the gallows prepared to die she was asked once more by Reverend Nicholas Noyes, assistant minister in the Salem church, to confess and thus save her immortal soul. Far from confessing, Good is said to have screamed, "You're a liar! I'm no more a witch than you are a wizard! If you take my life away, God will give you blood to drink!"

—*The Salem Witch Trials* by Marilynne K. Roach

CHAPTER 40

Gallows Hill

THE MORNING OF JULY 19 dawns bright and clear. From the prison cell, I can see the wisps of white clouds against the expanse of blue. A beautiful day in the town of Salem. The day of my ordered execution.

I slept little last night, and along with my cellmates, I broke out into tears many times. We huddled together, holding hands, realizing that these moments were the final moments that we'd feel flesh against flesh.

God has not abandoned us as I thought, for he encircled little Dorothy as she slept peacefully, covered with Elizabeth's warm shawl. Elizabeth would leave it now; she'd leave everything, as would the rest of us.

I gaze at the sleeping form of Dorothy and wonder what she will think when her mother leaves with the rest of us. What will she think when her mother doesn't return today, or tomorrow, or ever?

It may seem implausible to accuse a four-year-old of witchcraft, but the evidence sleeps just a few feet from me. I wonder how long she will remain in prison; she has no trial date set.

"Susannah," someone whispers my name, and I turn my head toward the voice. It's Rebecca, and she holds out her hand to me.

Reaching over, I grasp her hand, and then she bows her head and begins to pray.

I close my eyes along with the other women who have their heads bowed too. After a moment, I open my eyes and watch Rebecca's thin, colorless lips move in supplication.

Time has a way of slowing down when there are moments that can never be repeated. As Rebecca speaks her reverent words, Dorothy wakes up with alarm in her eyes. I am not sure what her mother has told her about today, but sometimes a child knows when danger is near.

Dorothy springs to her feet and scrambles to her mother's side. After all of the bonding I've shared with the little girl, Sarah Good is still her mother, first and foremost.

Sarah breaks off holding the other women's hands and pulls Dorothy on her lap. Sarah's eyes begin watering, which makes the tears fall on my own face.

In this moment, with the early morning light just barely peeking into our cell, Dorothy looks like her mother. The two heads are bent together in a tangle of matted knots. Sarah is whispering to her daughter, and then I realize that she is singing.

Elizabeth stops praying as Sarah's singing grows louder. I haven't heard Sarah sing before, but her voice is surprisingly sweet and clear. Perhaps all music had been forgotten since coming to this cell. As Sarah sings, Dorothy clings tighter to her, and the sun continues to rise until there seems to be a halo of gold surrounding the place where their heads are touching.

All too soon, the jailer opens the cell door. His guards

enter, their faces pulled into tight lines, ropes dangling from their hands.

Dorothy starts to scream, and I jolt upward with a start. Her mother has been taken out of the cell many times, yet Dorothy has never reacted like this. It's as if her four-year-old mind understands what is happening to her mother.

If I could pray for one last thing, it would be that Dorothy forgets these last few months as she grows older. That she will not have these horrible memories, especially of her mother being led away with her hands tied behind her back.

Sarah Good grabs Dorothy and shakes her. "Do not scream," she said, her own voice breaking. "You be a good girl. You be quiet and obedient."

Dorothy quiets, but she is still hiccupping on her sobs with tears streaming down her face. I know that if I hug or kiss her good-bye, it will be I who falls to screaming.

I turn away from mother and child and squeeze my eyes shut as they burn hot with tears. I can no longer watch the farewell between the two. I let my head fall forward and keep my gaze on the ground as I shuffle out of the prison cell for the last time. Elizabeth walks in front of me, Rebecca follows me, then Sarah Wildes, and finally, Sarah Good tears herself away from Dorothy and joins us in the corridor.

As the cell door shuts, I wait for Dorothy's screams to start up again, or crying, or anything. But instead, there is silence so heavy that it feels like a boulder is crushing my heart. At least my children are grown and I was able to raise all of them to adulthood.

The corridor is dark and filled with stench. I feel the eyes of the other prisoners on us as we pass by. One person laughs, but it's a maniacal laugh, one I've heard at random times before. A few voices call out farewell—although they are only whispers. Still I hear them. It seems I can hear every sound, every breath, even the beating of my own heart.

We step outside onto the streets of Salem. The sunlight is blinding, even though it is still morning. I have not felt it on my face for weeks, although it feels like years. The warmth touches my skin and surges through my body, cradling my heart. The sun's rays feel miraculous, as if the hand of God has reached down from Heaven, touching my skin one more time.

For after today, what will I feel, if anything?

The cart is waiting in the center of the square, and we walk toward it in near silence. Groups of people stand on the edges of the street, but I don't scan the faces to pick out anyone familiar. I have said my good-byes.

One by one, we are hoisted into the back of the cart that is littered with bits of hay. As the driver of the wagon climbs up on his perch, someone yells out, "Devil's spawn!"

And that's all it takes.

The people surround the cart, shouting and threatening, telling us we will burn in hell for our crimes.

For a moment, I miss the confines of our dank, dark cell, where we were locked away from verbal accusations. Now, we are in the open air, beneath the sun, but the angry voices crowd against our last moments of life.

The cart lurches forward, and we sway against each other. The journey to what they now call Gallows Hill is short, but each moment feels as long as a full day. My heart thuds in time with the pounding of the horses' hooves. I am perspiring beneath the heat of the sun, yet I feel chilled at the same time.

Rebecca Nurse bows her head and begins to pray, and soon we are all praying, the rumbling of our cart covering up our whispers. After a moment, I lift my head. People are waiting by the sides of the road, following the wagon as we reach them. Men, women, and children. I recognize faces, both from my trial and from Salisbury, the place I thought I'd live out my days.

When the cart travels up the incline of Gallows Hill and finally comes to a stop, I almost can't breathe. Is this really happening or am I dreaming the worst of nightmares? I watch the women around me as they are helped down from the cart and led to a platform built atop the rocky pinnacle. Hanging from an adjacent scaffold is a noose.

My throat tightens, and I want to claw off the ropes binding my wrists together. I want to run, but there is nowhere to go.

And then I see them. My children. They are to the right of the wooden platform, their faces ashen and pale. I look away, and then I turn my head back toward them, lifting my chin. They will see me hanged today, but they will witness my innocence.

Sarah Good is led to the platform, and I think of her daughter Dorothy, still confined to a prison cell. Reverend Nicholas Noyes waits near the scaffold, and as Sarah Good approaches, he says, "Admit your guilt so that you will not die a liar."

"I am not guilty," she says sharply.

Even I am surprised at the vehemence.

"You know you are a witch. The court has found you guilty, and you can no longer deny it," Reverend Noyes continues. "Confess it and cleanse your soul before you are hanged."

"*You* are a liar," Sarah says, her eyes narrowed and hard. "I am no more a witch than you are a wizard, and if you take away my life, God will give you blood to drink."

The reverend's eyes widen, and he lets Sarah take her

place without another word. I close my eyes as the rope is settled around Sarah's neck. I cannot see, and I cannot hear.

I step up onto the platform, and several in the crowd erupt into accusations. I am deaf to them now. I have said my last words, and no words are needed now. The executioner slides the rope over my head and across my face and chin. Then it is around my neck, and as it grows tight, I look out over the crowd.

Beyond the sad faces, beyond the jeering calls, I see someone who makes my heart swell.

George.

But it is not the man I imagined coming to my cell day after day to offer words of comfort. It is the man I met forty-six years ago. George's hair is dark, his shoulders broad, his back straight, and his smile . . . is exactly how I remember.

Even from where I am, looking over the gathered crowd, I see his gray eyes, like a calm ocean on a summer day. His gaze holds mine as he moves forward, coming through the crowd. It's as if they don't even exist, but somehow they step aside for him.

For a moment, I'm confused. Do they see him too? Is it possible that he's risen from the grave?

But the youth of his skin and the strength of his body tell me this is not a walking ghost, but my one and true George.

My mouth forms his name, and then I hear him speak.

"Susannah," he says, his voice carrying across to me and entering my heart. "I've come for you, my dear."

My eyes burn with tears, but they are tears of joy, not of sorrow.

He has come for me. Just as he said he would. He is only a few steps away when he lifts his hand.

I reach for him, watching the distance between our fingers close in until I have nearly touched him.

I am suddenly jerked away from his reach, just before he can touch me. My body swings cruelly away, and many in the crowd avert their eyes. But George is still there, his gaze steady.

He moves closer and closer, and when my body swings toward him again, he only smiles softly and waits.

It doesn't take long for the breath to leave my body, coursing through my lungs one last time, then ebbing out in spurts. And as my breath fades into nothingness, my hand connects with George's, and our fingers thread together.

I look behind me, at the hanging body that was once mine—now the body of an old and broken woman, who lived a good many years, most of them in happiness, taking care of children, my parents, and my George. But even as the good memories of a lifetime swirl around me, I know that I will spend eternity forgetting these past three months of hell.

Looking into George's eyes, tears spill from my eyes. I didn't know it was possible to cry when one has died, but it seems the emotions are still real and full.

"Susannah," he says, pulling me into his arms.

I dissolve into him, and we stand there for many moments. I no longer hear the crowds, I no longer see my silent empty body, and I no longer feel the pain.

All I can see and hear now is my loving George.

And then I know. I have arrived in Paradise at last.

The Witch's Daughter
"Let Goody Martin rest in peace,
I never knew her to harm a fly,
And witch or not – God knows – not I?
I know who swore her life away;
And as God lives, I'd not condemn
An Indian dog on word of them."

—John Greenleaf Whittier, 1857
Direct descendant of Susannah Martin

AUTHOR'S NOTE

For the purposes of the story and the interactions between the prisoners, I have placed them in close proximity to each other. This is a brief summary of their actual locations and arrest dates:

Susannah North Martin: age 71, arrested April 30, 1692. She was held in Salem Jail, then hanged in Salem at Gallows Hill on July 19, 1692.

Sarah Good: age 39, arrested March 1, 1692, held in Ipswich, then moved to Salem Jail on March 5. She was tried in Salem Town House, and hanged in Salem on July 19, 1692.

Mercy Good: infant daughter of Sarah Good. Mercy was born in jail, and later died in jail sometime before July 19, 1692. Boston prison warden John Arnold spent ten shillings to provide two blankets for Mercy.

Dorothy (Dorcas) Good: age 4, daughter of Sarah Good. Dorothy was arrested March 24, 1692, and held in Salem Jail with her mother. She was released from jail December 10, 1692 on £50 bond. She never recovered mentally.

Elizabeth How(e): age 57, arrested May 28, 1692, held in Boston Jail, then transferred to Salem Jail. She was tried in Salem and hanged on Gallows Hill on July 19, 1692.

Rebecca Nurse: age 71, accused March 12, 1692, arrested March 23. She was held in Salem Jail and despite a petition of thirty-five people protesting her charges, she was hanged on July 19, 1692.

Sarah Wildes: age 65, arrested April 21, 1692. She was held in Salem Prison and hanged on July 19, 1692.

Roger Toothaker: age 58, arrested May 18, 1692, held in Boston Prison. Later transferred to Salem Jail where he died on June 16, 1692.

Bridget Bishop: age 60, arrested April 19. Held in Salem Jail. She was the first woman hanged in Salem, June 10, 1692.

No historical records reveal what the first accusation was against Susannah Martin in 1647 or 1648. She was fined twenty shillings, and her seat placement in the Meeting House changed. Her husband, George, objected to her seat placement, which he probably felt was below her status in the community. In this story, I've recreated a conflict in order to satisfy the demands of this event.

ACKNOWLEDGEMENTS

As with all works of historical fiction, the research efforts are immense. With this story in particular, I knew I had to satisfy seasoned historians and family records that spanned across generations. This is why I decided not to focus so much on the accusations and the trial proceedings, because I felt those did not need to be duplicated. Instead, I focused on the life and loves of Susannah North Martin. While researching her history, I was struck by the impression that she and her husband had an incredibly strong marriage and a prodigious love for each other. Time and time again, George defended Susannah in court against various accusations. They raised nine children together. They loved and lost, rejoiced and grieved, and despite the volatile community in which they raised their family, in the end, they triumphed over what any court of law might accuse them of. Susannah went to her death on Gallows Hill with a clear conscience, ready to meet her Maker and to be reunited with her dear George.

This novel has been a work in progress since early 2012. Many thanks to my readers and support network over the past five years: Mindy Holt, Taffy Lovell, Jeff Savage, Robison Wells, Annette Lyon, Michele Paige Holmes, Sarah Eden, Lu Ann Staheli, Jaime Theler, Theresa Sneed, Julianne Clegg, and Gayle Brown, who all contributed to the production of this manuscript in various ways. I'm grateful for my agent, Jane Dystel, and her faith in me. And I'm grateful to editor Jennie Stevens who helped fine-tune the story and made some amazing "saves". Thanks as well to proofreader Corey Pulver, photographer Brekke Felt, model

Dana Moore, cover designer Rachael Anderson, and formatter Heather Justesen. My stories would be black ink on plain white paper without the talents of so many. And finally, thanks to my husband and children and my extended family, and especially my father, Scott Kent Brown, whose lineage descends from Susannah Martin.

ABOUT HEATHER B. MOORE

HEATHER B. MOORE writes historical thrillers under the pen name H.B. Moore; her latest thrillers include *Slave Queen* and *The Killing Curse*. Under the name Heather B. Moore, she writes romance and women's fiction; her newest releases are the *USA Today* bestseller *Heart of the Ocean* and the historical romance *Love is Come*. She's also one of the coauthors of the *USA Today* bestselling series: A Timeless Romance Anthology.

For book updates, sign up for Heather's email list:
hbmoore.com/contact
Website: HBMoore.com
Facebook: Fans of H. B. Moore
Blog: MyWritersLair.blogspot.com
Instagram: @authorhbmoore
Twitter: @HeatherBMoore

RESEARCH REFERENCES

Family Search "Susannah North Martin: Witch Trial Story" https://familysearch.org/photos/stories/1240545 Web access: January 2015

Find a Grave "George Martin" http://www.findagrave.com/cgibin/fg.cgi?page=gr&GRid=43 226990 Web access: January 2015

Find a Grave "Susannah North Martin" http://www.findagrave.com/cgi-bin/fg.cgi?page=gr&GRid=8292 Web access: January 2015

Geni "Susannah Martin (North)" http://www.geni.com/people/SusannahMartin/60000000036 15754555 Web access: January 2015

History of American Women "Elizabeth Howe" http://www.womenhistoryblog.com/2008/05/elizabeth-jackson-howe.html Web access: January 2015

History of American Women "Sarah Wildes" http://www.womenhistoryblog.com/2008/05/sarah-averill-wildes.html Web access: January 2015

History of Massachusetts "Susannah Martin: Accused Witch of Salisbury" http://historyofmassachusetts.org/susannah-martin-accused-witch-from-salisbury/ Web access: January 2015

History of Massachusetts "The Trial of Rebecca Nurse"
http://historyofmassachusetts.org/the-trial-of-rebecca-nurse/
Web access: January 2015

History.com "This Day in History"
http://www.history.com/this-day-in-history/first-salem-witch-hanging Web access: January 2015

Legends of America "Elizabeth Howe"
http://www.legendsofamerica.com/ma-witches-h.html   Web access: January 2015

Legends of America "Rebecca Nurse"
http://www.legendsofamerica.com/ma-witches-k-n.html
Web access: January 2015

Miner Descent "Richard North"
http://minerdescent.com/2010/10/27/richard-north/
Web access: January 2015

Legends of America "Roger Toothaker"
http://www.legendsofamerica.com/ma-witches-t.html
Web access: January 2015

Legends of America "Sarah Good"
http://www.legendsofamerica.com/ma-witches-f-g.html
Web access: January 2015

Legends of America "Sarah Wildes"
http://www.legendsofamerica.com/ma-witches-u-z.html
Web access: January 2015

Legends of America "Susannah North Martin"
http://www.legendsofamerica.com/ma-witches-k-n.html
Web access: January 2015

New England Families "Susannah Martin"
http://nefamilies.com/fam/groupsheetI100002806.aspx
Web access: January 2015

Roots Web "Depositions"
http://www.rootsweb.ancestry.com/~nwa/atk.html
Web access: January 2015

Roots Web "Susannah North Martin"
http://www.rootsweb.com/~nwa/sm.html
Web access: January 2015

Salem Witch Trials Documentary Archive and Transcription
"Bridget Bishop"
http://salem.lib.virginia.edu/people?mbio.num=mb1
Web access: January 2015

Salem Witch Trials Documentary Archive and Transcription
"Project Search the Salem Witch Trial Papers"
http://salem.lib.virginia.edu/texts/salemSearch.htm?rows=10
&start=0&field_limit=tei&q=Susannah+Martin&query=mar
sus_Web access: January 2015

Salem Witch Trials Documentary Archive and Transcription
"Rebecca Nurse"
http://salem.lib.virginia.edu/people?group.num=all&mbio.n
um=mb21 Web access: January 2015

Salem Witch Trials Documentary Archive and Transcription "Salem Village Witchcraft Victims' Memorial at Danvers" Salem Witch Trials Documentary Archive and Transcription. Web access: January 2015

Salem Witch Trials Documentary Archive and Transcription "Sarah Good" http://salem.lib.virginia.edu/people/good.html Web access: January 2015

Salem Witch Trials Documentary Archive and Transcription "Sarah Osborne"
http://salem.lib.virginia.edu/people/osborne.html Web access: January 2015

Salem Witch Trials Documentary Archive and Transcription "Susannah Martin"
http://salem.lib.virginia.edu/people?group.num=all&mbio.num=mb17 Web access: January 2015

The Salem Witch Trials: A Day-to-Day Chronicle of a Community Under Siege, by Marilynne K. Roach. Taylor Trade Publishing. October 25, 2004.

Wikipedia "Susannah Martin"
http://en.wikipedia.org/wiki/Susannah_Martin
Web access: January 2015

Wiki Tree "Mary (North) Jones"
http://www.wikitree.com/wiki/North-171
Web access: January 2015

Made in the USA
San Bernardino, CA
19 March 2017